Minerva Clark

goes to the dogs

Also by Karen Karbo

Minerva Clark Gets a Clue

MINERVA CLARK

goes to the dogs

BY KAREN KARBO

SCHOLASTIC INC.
New York Toronto London Auckland Sydney
Mexico City New Delhi Hong Kong Buenos Aires

ISBN-13: 978-0-439-93420-6
ISBN-10: 0-439-93420-6

12 11 10 9 8 7 6 5 4 3 2 1   7 8 9 10 11 12/0

Printed in the U.S.A.   40

First Scholastic printing, April 2007

Typeset in Westchester Book Composition

For Fiona,
again and always

- 1 -

I defy you to find a more disgusting chore than cleaning out the refrigerator at my house. My three older brothers believe in leftovers, except when it comes to eating them.

Cleaning out the fridge was my job, even though I don't believe in leftovers *at all.* I took out the Tupperware containing mysterious fuzz-covered blobs, white take-out cartons half full of rotting Who Knows What, and plastic bags of mushy fruit and set them on the counter.

I wished I could become a superhero for three minutes, so that I could pick the fridge up, fly it to the closest Dumpster, and empty out the entire thing. But no. Mark Clark, my oldest older brother, who's been basically in charge of things since my parents got divorced, had to peek inside all the containers before deciding what stayed and what went, even though in the end it all went. What a system.

I sighed. I took my cell out of my back pocket, checked to see if I'd missed any calls. At first I thought my summer would rock because my parents weren't around—my mom had moved to Santa Fe to teach yoga with her weird boyfriend, Rolando, and my dad, Charlie, was always out of town on business—but Mark Clark was turning out to be worse than any parent. He had attacks of guilt where he thought I was going to be scarred for life, so he gave me extra chores and extra rules and signed me up for special classes that were supposed to help me get into a good college, which would prove I was not scarred at all.

At the bottom of one of the vegetable crisper drawers, in the way back, I found a plastic bag of radishes that had been in there so long the frilly green tops had turned into a gooey pale brown liquid. I picked up the top of the plastic bag with two fingers, dragged it out, and flung it into the garbage. Some of the rotted radish top goop got on my hands.

"Disgusting!" I shrieked to the empty kitchen.

It was late in the morning. The brothers were all out. Maybe it was the sweet/sour smell that got worse the closer I got to the back of the fridge, or maybe I was PMSing, but tears started in my eyes. It was the first time I'd cried since the electric shock that changed my life, where for reasons even the doctors could not explain, my self-consciousness and self-loathing had been jolted clean out of my head. Or else the electricity had somehow rewired my brain, so that I came to feel that while no, I wasn't perfect, I was fine just the way I was. They kept saying it was a mystery, the way the brain worked. My friend Hannah said the shock had turned me into the Queen of Self-Esteem. Whatever.

The moral of the story is, even if you are the Queen of Self-Esteem, life can still suck. I know I know I know. Life is unfair. My brothers tell me that all the time. But only the month before, I'd solved a real murder case *and* helped crack a major identity theft ring, and now here I was stuck doing boring summer chores, just like any stupid kid. But I've found out the hard way that just because you solve one mystery, that doesn't mean the cops or newspaper writers or whoever will automatically call your cell and ask for your help.

Quills, my second-oldest older brother, always says people are afraid to color outside the lines, and an example of this is grown-ups refusing to see how handy it would be to have a thirteen-year-old on your case squad or working for your detective agency. The people being investigated would get one look at my braces and girl-raised-by-wolves hair and high-tops and think I was just a dorky kid who couldn't possibly know a thing. I could wander through the world like a distracted teen and be sleuthing the whole time. I could ask questions that would seem dumb or rude coming from an adult, and no one would suspect a thing.

But no one was interested.

It's not like I haven't been trying.

I called 911 with information about a suspicious-looking character in our neighborhood who wore a knit ski cap and parka in ninety-degree weather and went up and down the street on garbage day, picking through the recycle bins for bottles. I also called about the house next door that got TPed by boys I recognized from my school, Holy Family. I was pretty sure the paper had been stolen from the school's supply closet, since they'd done it once before. I called about a tricycle I saw in a tree at the end of the block. How did it get there? And wasn't some rug rat crying his eyes out because it was missing?

The same operator always seemed to answer the phone when I called. She had a deep musical voice like those old-timey blues singer ladies that my dad sometimes listened to. The last time I called (about the tricycle in the tree) she said, "Minerva Clark, you are a kick in the pants, girl, but you need to use the regular number and stop dialing 911."

I asked, "Kick in the pants how exactly?"

"You be good now," said the operator. Then I heard the click in my ear.

I was trying to figure out whether I'd get in trouble for using a dish towel to sop up the dead radish goop at the back of the crisper drawer when my cell rang. I held my breath, said a little prayer to whatever saint oversees the boyfriend-girlfriend situation, and flipped open the phone without checking the number. I wanted it to be Kevin, who I met while I was solving my last mystery. Kevin. He was taller than me. He had crunchy shiny swimmer's hair and blue eyes and dark eyebrows. A hottie extraordinaire. Extraordinaire is French for extraordinary.

I'd invited Kevin to the last dance of the year. We slow-danced every slow dance, and he told me he liked my wild hair, that surfer girls on the island of Maui had hair just like mine. Then, the day after school got out he left on vacation with his parents, which is where he was right now. At the dance, he bought me a Dr Pepper from the snack table using his own money. I didn't let myself think about it too much—I thought about it all the time! I could hardly think of anything else!—but I wondered if he would be my boyfriend, if he wasn't in Montana fly-fishing.

But the call wasn't from Kevin. It was someone who normally never called me, except once in the sixth grade, when she was having a slumber party and wanted to make sure I got the point that I hadn't been invited.

"Minerva, I didn't know who else to call. I need some help, like right now. I thought about how, since you're so good at solving mysteries and everything, maybe you could help me. I lost a ring and I need to find it immediately. I am so in trouble. My dad wants to kill me. I hate it when my dad wants to kill me."

The voice was familiar, but it was hard to tell who it was because she was sniffling and hiccupping, gulping down air as if they weren't making any more of it. "Who *is* this?" I asked.

"It's Chelsea. De Guzman? From your class?" She sounded irritated that she had to identify herself, like rich people sometimes do when you ask them normal questions. "I've got to get the ring back tonight, or sooner. As soon as possible. I am so busted. I am in so much trouble." She tried to catch her breath.

"Okay," I said. I closed the crisper drawer. Someone would go to the grocery store soon and toss a new bag of carrots in there and no one would ever see the dead radish goop puddle in the back. I grabbed a can of Mountain Dew, closed the refrigerator door, and sat right down there on the kitchen floor to listen to Chelsea's story.

The day after school got out, Chelsea went to London

with her mom and dad. Chelsea is an only child and her mom is one of those moms who always has perfect hair and fingernails and helps out at school, and her dad is Louis de Guzman Fine Jewelry. If you live here in Portland, you know his name, but I think he also has shops in fancy places like Beverly Hills. The de Guzmans live in one of those giant mansions on Knott Avenue that take up an entire block and have pillars and balconies and a Japanese gardener out front pinching off the tiny dead azalea flowers, one by one.

Chelsea and her parents were at the airport with their matching luggage, loopy tired from the eight-hundred-hour flight from London. It was a little after 10:00 A.M. They'd been flying all night. Chelsea wanted a cappuccino. Chelsea was the kind of girl who drank cappuccino and got manicures and wore ankle bracelets. I don't like coffee just yet, although somewhere along the way kids start drinking coffee. In my opinion this, and not taking out the garbage without being asked, is the first sign of being a grown-up.

Chelsea said she would die if she did not have a cappuccino, but her parents just wanted to get home. Chelsea begged, and they gave in, but said that she needed to be down in the baggage claim area at 10:30 sharp, or else they were going home without her. Chelsea was a well-known dawdler.

She got in line at a small coffee place on the main

concourse called Coffee People. She said the line was all the way out the door. She said she must have waited an hour, standing there staring into the fingerprint-smeared glass case of scones and muffins. But of course she couldn't have waited an hour, because her parents had given her about twenty minutes.

The lady ahead of her sighed a lot and folded her arms, and kept switching her weight from one hip to the other, all impatient. She had waist-length hair, thick and coarse like a horse's tail, and she kept swishing it around. "This is so ridiculous," said the lady to no one in particular. She had an accent, but not like the de Guzmans' housekeeper, Agata. Maybe the lady was Hispanic? Then she turned and asked Chelsea the time. Chelsea looked at her phone. It was 10:15.

"She asked to see my ring—you know that flower ring I got at Claire's? All the popular girls wanted one, remember? That totally adorable one, with the silver band and the little crystals that formed the petals around the bigger pink crystal? Remember? I wore it to the dance."

"Not really," I said. *In case you didn't notice, I was totally into that guy I was slow-dancing with,* I wanted to say, but didn't. "So you showed her the ring."

"For only six bucks it was really the cutest ring. Very girly, but it would still look good on someone like you. Wait. That sounds really bad. I didn't mean it to sound bad."

I laughed. "So you showed her the ring."

"Are you *secretly* hating me right now?"

"Yeah, Chelsea, I'm secretly hating you. Except now you know, so it's not a secret." I rolled my eyes, even though there was no one around to appreciate it.

"Don't tease me. I've had a terrible day." She sniffled.

"So the lady in line ahead of you wanted to check out your ring."

"She wasn't a lady exactly. More kind of probably twenty or something. Not old, but not a teenager either. She was wearing this awful awful purple tunic-y thing over jeans with a studded belt on the *outside.* Anyway, she asked if she could try it on and I said sure, and she tried it on and then she said she'd give me fifty dollars for it."

"For your *ring* from *Claire's?*" My tone said: Only a crazy person would offer fifty bucks for one of those cheap, cut-glass rings from Claire's, world headquarters for the type of cheesy jewelry and hair ornaments girls my age can't resist.

"Yeah, I know. What was up with that? I thought she was joking at first, but she wasn't. She really really loved it. She said she was all into flowers, especially daisies, and she'd been wanting a ring like this just for forever, but could never find one. I thought I was being really smart."

"So the girl gave you fifty bucks? Just like that?"

"Yep. Two twenties and a ten. I could buy *five* rings with that money. My dad is always hammering me about how you should never let opportunity pass you by and that's what I thought I was doing, and then when we were in the cab on the way home my dad asked where my ring was. He picked up my hand and saw it wasn't there and freaked out. He started yelling at me right there in the cab and cussing and that big vein in his forehead stuck out and his face was so red I thought he was going to have a heart attack, like he's had before, you know my dad had that heart attack? When we were in fourth grade? I didn't get to sing my solo in the Christmas pageant? Anyway, we're in the cab and my dad's screaming at me, and my mom's screaming at my dad to calm down and then he's like complaining about chest pains and my mom makes the driver go straight to the hospital."

"Is your dad okay?"

"The doctor said it was anxiety or something. They didn't tell me. They just said he wasn't having another heart attack, and it was a good thing for *me*."

"The doctors said that?"

"No no no," said Chelsea impatiently. "I'm saying that. I'm just lucky I didn't give my dad a heart attack over this." Chelsea had gotten herself worked up again. She cried and hiccupped and sniffled some more. Then I heard her take a long deep breath in an attempt to get herself together.

"Why was he so mad?" I asked.

"Probably because I'm always losing stuff. I'm already on my third cell phone."

"But you didn't lose the ring, you sold it."

"I said I lost it. I didn't want him to get even madder. As it is he's already probably going to ground me off the computer for the rest of the summer. And I know lying's bad and stuff, and we're not supposed to do it, ever, but I'm glad I did. Because it turns out I messed up royally. It turns out my dad had replaced the glass stone in the center of my Claire's ring with a red diamond."

"A red diamond? You mean, like a real gem?" This didn't make any sense to me.

"He does it all the time when he's bringing gems into the country. It's too expensive to hire a company to transport it and you have to insure it and a whole bunch of things that are really expensive, I don't know, I don't *know* why he does it! Sometimes I think it's just to show how smart he is. While we were in London he bought a red diamond for some important piece of jewelry he's making for someone, and he took the cut glass out of the center of my ring and replaced it with the diamond. He thought it would be easy to get it home that way. Easier and cheaper."

"You *sold* some lady a ring with a real diamond in it?" My heart was a bongo played by a mad gorilla.

"Nobody told me he'd made the switch. My mom

told me afterward. At the hospital. I didn't know. They thought if I knew, I'd wreck it. And look, I did wreck it."

"How much is this red diamond worth?"

"I don't know. Red diamonds are super rare. Millions maybe?"

"Millions?"

Chelsea de Guzman was a known drama queen. At the end of last year, when we got to watch *Seabiscuit* as a reward for not throwing pencils at each other in Mass, Chelsea had to go to the nurse because she was so upset when Seabiscuit broke his leg or tore his tendon or whatever it was that made him lame. I doubted the red diamond—who'd even heard of such a thing?—was worth millions. Still, the whole situation was pretty strange.

"Didn't your dad call the police, or airport security, or whatever?"

"I don't know. I think my mom called someone. There wasn't any time. Pretty much the minute he found out the ring was gone his chest pains started. So can you help me? I still have the fifty dollars. If we could just find her, I'll give her the money back. I'll give her sixty dollars, even. I just have to get that ring back."

"I have to finish this thing I'm doing, then I'll call you back. In the meantime, you sit down and think if there was anything else special about the girl, besides her long dark hair."

Chelsea begged me to give an exact time when I would call her back. I said as soon as possible. I needed to give this whole thing some thought.

I had only two shelves to go in the fridge, the top ones where we keep the milk and jars of olives and mayonnaise. I threw out a jar of olive juice that probably hadn't had olives in it since Christmas, the last time I performed this chore. I wiped down the glass shelves with a sponge.

It was just plain weird for a stranger to offer to buy a cheap ring right off your finger. Then again, one time a lady in the canned fruits aisle at the grocery store offered to buy my purple Chuck Taylors right off my feet. I said no way, but thank you very much. What was I going to do, walk around in my holey socks? So the main question was: Why did a strange woman want to buy Chelsea's ring?

Chelsea and I have known each other since pre-K, but I didn't know her well. The closest we'd come were friends of friends of friends. These were the things I knew about Chelsea de Guzman: She was the only girl in our class who always wore a skirt on Free Dress Day. She was the only girl who got an A in algebra. Her family had a bunch of money and a bunch of those dogs called corgis, the same kind the Queen of England has. She was commonly thought to be the second-cutest girl in our class, after my friend Hannah. She was someone you always said you liked and thought was sweet and nice, so that she wouldn't start a mean rumor about you.

After I finished with the fridge, I closed the door and stared at the notes each brother had left stuck to the door beneath a magnet. The magnets were life-size pictures of creepy things. Beneath a red-legged tarantula was an orange Post-it saying Mark Clark was at work, would be home around five o'clock. Beneath a black beetle was a scrap of notebook paper saying Quills was out auditioning new drummers for Humongous Bag of Cashews, then going to look at a new guitar, would be home before six o'clock. Beneath a caterpillar was a yellow Post-it saying Morgan was doing some yard work for one of his college professors and would be home before donkeys could fly. Har!

Each note also listed the best number at which to reach each brother. The notes were Mark Clark's idea. It was the first summer I'd be left alone most of the day. Thirteen is a well-known awkward age, too old for a babysitter and too young to have a summer job.

When no one was home, Casa Clark felt enormous. We called it Casa Clark because, unlike every other old wood-shingled bungalow on our street, ours was a stucco box that looks like a Mexican restaurant. It used to be pink, but before my parents got a divorce they painted it light brown. It has three floors and a brass fireman's pole that went from the third floor straight into the kitchen, which I used to love as a kid, but now is sort of an embarrassment. I don't know why.

I woke Jupiter up from his nap. Jupiter is my ferret. His cage is kept behind the grand piano in the living room. He was dead asleep, snoring inside a black denim pants leg. Jupiter loves nothing more than sleeping inside a pants leg. He has a whole assortment of pants-leg sleeping tubes, and as a result my brothers and I have a whole assortment of cutoffs.

I tried to cuddle Jupiter under my chin, but he threw himself out of my arms and ran across the hall to the dining room. He took three mad laps around our big table, leaped on a chair, then onto the table, where he knocked over a near-empty carton of milk that had been sitting there since breakfast. It spilled onto the open newspaper.

I stared at the empty red and white carton, lying on its side. The sight of the milk-soaked newspaper gave me an idea. I tugged my phone from my back pocket and punched in Chelsea's number, scooped Jupiter up, and dropped him back into his cage. He didn't like this at all. He thought we were going to play, and we were, until the spilled milk gave me an idea.

"Chelsea, it's me, Minerva Clark. The girl who bought your ring, you said she was in line in front of you at the coffee place?"

"Yeah, why?"

"What did she order and how did she pay?"

"What did she order? Coffee. That's why it's called Coffee People. 'Cause people buy coffee there." She giggled for no reason. Like many girls in our grade, Chelsea had a laugh that sounded practiced.

"Just a cup of coffee? Not a latte or something more complicated?"

"Complicated how?"

"You know." I started feeling a mood coming on. Was Chelsea being dense on purpose? "Like a half-caf, half-decaf soy macchiato, extra hot."

"She did, actually. I remember because I started feeling totally tweaked that it took her so long to explain exactly what she wanted. It was already almost ten thirty."

"How did she pay?"

"With money?"

"Did she use a card? A credit or debit card?"

"Definitely. One of those. There was some something about the receipt. She gave the cashier person the wrong one and they traded. Then she threw it away anyway."

"You saw her throw it away? You're sure?"

"Positive. I remember being at amazed at how long her hair was. And the only time she was standing with her back to me was when she was at the garbage can, sticking the receipt through the little flap thingy."

"I thought you said she was in front of you."

I could practically hear Chelsea roll her eyes. "She *was*. But we were too busy talking about my ring for me to notice, you know?"

"Perfectimento. I know how we can find her. Meet me at the airport in half an hour."

- 2 -

Chelsea did not want to go to the airport. She was exhausted. Her mom had just dropped her at home, then gone straight back to the hospital. How was she supposed to get to the airport, anyway? Chelsea was a girl full of excuses for why something couldn't happen. Maybe this had to do with being good in algebra, at which yours truly sucked beyond belief.

I told her there was a good chance that the name of the lady who bought her ring was at the airport, and if she wanted to find her, we had to go now. We didn't have a minute to waste. I told her to take MAX, and meet me at the airport in front of Page and Turner Books on the main concourse at 1:00.

Chelsea said she'd never been on MAX, which was completely untrue since I remembered at least three times our class took MAX downtown on a field trip. MAX stood for Metropolitan Area Express, and was a teenager's best friend. You could get anywhere you needed to go around town on MAX, and it was well lit and completely safe and had no more bad smells than you would encounter on the city bus. Chelsea whined that she didn't know where the closest MAX station was ("My family doesn't really *do* public transportation"), or how much it cost, plus how was she supposed to sneak out of the house?

"Chelsea," I said, "if you can't figure out how to sneak out of your own house, then I can't help you."

Then I hung up on her. Chelsea would think up one excuse after another if I didn't just put an end to the conversation by hanging up, a technique I learned from watching detective shows with Quills. He is such a fan of *Law & Order* he taught himself to play the theme song on his bass. The phone calls are very short on that show, in case you haven't noticed.

I changed out of my jean cutoffs and black Green Day T-shirt into a pair of jeans that hadn't been cut off yet and another Green Day T-shirt and slid my feet into my new turquoise Chuck Taylor high-tops, which I'd supposedly got to replace my purple ones, but here is a secret about Chuck Taylors—you never replace the old ones, they are just retired to the back of the closet. I stuck my hair on top of my head, brushed my teeth, made sure I had my house keys—I am dead meat if I forget my house keys and have to call one of the brothers—grabbed my hoodie, and set out down the hill toward the MAX station.

On the way, I called Mark Clark to let him know I was going over to my friend Chelsea's for a while. Technically I was going to the airport to help my friend Chelsea, but Mark Clark didn't need to know this. He would only worry. Our house rule was: When no one was home I could leave as long as I called the Brother-in-Charge and let him know where I was going. As long as I locked the house up properly and was home at the time I gave, no one asked questions. Or not more than about fifty, anyway.

The sun was a pale gray ball high in the sky behind the dull clouds. Still, it was warm, and all the roses were in bloom. That's how you know summer has arrived in Portland—it's warm and cloudy instead of cool and cloudy. I walked along, swinging my arms, glad to be out of the house. I tried not to feel deprived because I was the only girl my age on the planet who did not have an iPod. I also tried not to think about Kevin. I didn't think it was good for my sleuthing to be obsessed with someone who was only my almost-boyfriend. Anyway, he was coming home next Friday, 168 hours, give or take.

Suddenly, I heard a strangled screech. I looked up to see a hawk with a brown-spotted underside flying low overhead, with something in its talons—a small opossum or a rat that was cranking its skinny tail round and round in fear.

I slammed my eyes shut and pulled my hoodie up over my head. I couldn't stand the image of that little creature being carried away. I hated hated *hated* birds. Every few years I had a terrible bird experience. My first memory of a bird was in preschool. I got bit on my pointer finger by a duck while trying to feed it a piece of stale French bread. A few years later there was a chicken at some petting zoo that pecked at the back of my hair. Then there was that scary movie called *The Birds* that I watched at my friend Hannah's birthday slumber party one year. I don't know why we were allowed to watch it. It's an old movie from a time long ago when men and women used to dress up every day just to walk around. Birds invade a town and break into homes and peck out people's eyes. If I ever wanted to give myself a good shiver just for something to do, I thought about that stupid movie.

Even though the hawk was now just a speck in the sky, gliding away over the gray roofs, I sprinted down a cross street in the opposite direction, hoping he was too busy with his baby opossum to notice me. I ran as far as I could with my eyes closed, in case he decided to circle back and peck my eyes out.

I was sweaty from running, especially my scalp. I tied

my hair in a knot. We Clarks are a family of sweaty heads. Even Morgan, who is my youngest older brother and has the thinnest hair of all of us, gets a bad sweaty head from time to time. I wished I'd left my hoodie at home. I took it off and tied it tight around my waist. At the MAX station I sat down on a bench to wait.

No one I knew paid much attention to other people's parents. They all faded together: a bunch of old people who complained about their aching knees and listened to National Public Radio in the car. I did remember Mr. de Guzman, though. At the last parent/teacher conference of the year, Chelsea had the slot before me. The conferences were held in the cafeteria at card tables set in a long row. Unlike all the other dads, who showed up in business-casual khakis or jeans, Mr. de Guzman wore a suit and a red tie. He made notes on Chelsea's papers with a gold pen. He looked much more serious and rich than the rest of our parents. He was intimidating.

I found a seat on the train beside a lady in a black jacket and black pants, her roller suitcase tucked in front of her feet, tapping madly on her Palm Pilot. She was a businesswoman on the way to go on a business trip, obviously. That's one thing about MAX—you can always tell what people are up to by what they're wearing and what they're carrying. I found a stale Starburst in my back pocket. If there's one thing I like more than

a stale piece of red licorice, it's a stale kiwi banana Starburst. It's my favorite candy, hands down.

The airport is only twenty minutes from our house,
and MAX lets you off right at the terminal. The doors
whooshed open, and people hurrying to catch their
flights swarmed around me. I was early. I could take
my time. I'd told Chelsea to meet me in front of Page
and Turner Books on the main concourse. At our
airport—and maybe at all airports—there are a lot of
fancy shops selling expensive stationery, jewelry and
glass bowls, carved wooden animals, woolen blankets,
work-out clothes. Stuff you would never need to take
with you on an airplane. Page and Turner was almost
exactly across the way from Coffee People.

It was 1:10, then it was 1:20. I listened over the loud-
speaker to one boarding announcement after the next. It
was 1:30. There was a table stacked with books on sale
in front of the store, which I thumbed through for half
a lifetime. Inside the shop, the lady behind the register
kept glancing out the window at me, as if I was going to
steal something. A man who smelled like beer stood
staring at the display in the window, then dabbed his
eyes with his knuckles and wandered away. I kept looking over at Coffee People, to see how my plan was going
to work.

I told myself that if Chelsea wasn't here by 2:00 I was
leaving, but then there she was, hurrying toward me in

23

her lime green platform flip-flops, holding her dark blond hair to the sides of her head. It was wet. There were two fresh Band-Aids on her suntan legs, from where it looked like she cut herself shaving. She wore a pink and green flowered pleated skirt and a faded pink T-shirt that said PUGS NOT DRUGS across the front, over a picture of a tough-looking pug. She wore rubber bracelets and a couple of gold necklaces and smelled like lemon and vanilla and in general looked as if she was going to a dance and not to the airport to dig through the garbage, which was part of my plan.

Of course, Chelsea didn't know that yet.

"I was starting to think you weren't coming." I was surprised at how relieved I was to see her. The idea of trudging back home without having a new mystery to solve depressed me. I thought of an entire summer of boring chores and notes from my brothers tacked to the refrigerator.

"Sorry I'm late." She dug into her tiny green leather purse for some lip gloss, which she rolled on her already-glossy lips. "Did you get the ring?"

"Uh . . . no?" Chelsea apparently thought I would just magically produce it. She wanted the ring found, but she wanted it delivered special delivery right to her front door. "We're here to find the name of the lady who bought it from you. We need to figure out who has it before we can get it."

"Oh. Right." She sighed, patted her hair. "You're such a brainiac these days, I thought maybe you'd gotten it all figured out while you were waiting. Well, now what?"

"Now we go into Coffee People and hope they haven't emptied the garbage since you were here a few hours ago. You said the lady bought her drink with a credit card. See that big metal garbage can across from the counter where you pick up your drinks? Was that the can where you saw her throw away her receipt?"

I tipped my head toward Coffee People. Through the glass doors that opened up onto the concourse you could see everything: the glass pastry case, with its small piles of scones, cookies, and Danishes; the curved counter; and beside it, a tall stainless steel garbage can, into which a customer was slipping the wrapper from a straw.

"Yeah," said Chelsea. She wasn't looking at Coffee People at all, but was staring at me with the same fearful look you get when a teacher asks to see you after class.

"Here's the great thing. Coffee People's got their orders all computerized. I've been watching. It's not like Starbucks, where they call out the drinks. Watch the girl take the orders. She taps it into the cash register, then it pops up on the display by the coffee machine. Whatever complicated drink the lady ordered is probably written on the slip, along with the time she ordered it, which was sometime between ten o'clock and ten thirty, right?"

"Minerva, I am not going to go through the garbage."

"How else are we going to find the receipt?"

"What kind of a freak do you think I am? What if someone from *school,* saw us? Uhn-uh. No way." Her voice got louder and higher. A few passengers hurrying by on their way to the security gate turned and stared.

"I kind of doubt anyone from school will see us," I said.

"I know you might not care, because you think you're all cool and perfect at all times, or whatever it was that happened to you when you got electrocuted, but I still care what people think."

"I care what people think," I said.

"Fine. Whatever. But I am *not* digging through the garbage. I'll do anything else but that."

"All right," I said. "You distract the counter girl, while I take out the garbage bag."

She threw me a look.

"All you have to do is order something and spill it."

"Like what, a cup of coffee? No way. What if I get some on my skirt? I just got this skirt. It's from London."

"They have milk shakes, too. They're thicker, they won't splash."

"This is unbelievably stupid," said Chelsea, checking her phone to see if she had any messages.

"Come on, Chelsea. While I was waiting I watched the counter girl. She likes things neat. She wipes down the counter every time she gets a spare minute. Just watch her."

Chelsea and I looked over. The girl had just finished filling the napkin holder and was wiping it down with a white towel. A flight must have just arrived, because suddenly a herd of people with backpacks and roller suitcases formed themselves into a line.

As we watched, one of the airport janitors shuffled up with his trolley of cleaning supplies. He parked it just outside Coffee People, then strode inside. He said hey to the girl behind the counter. Even from this distance I could tell he was trying to impress her. He talked a lot, but she just nodded. He had a pair of sunglasses on top of his head. He took them off and showed them to her. A clear plastic bag stuck out of his back pocket. She started wiping down the counter with the white towel. He turned, lifted the lid off the can with one hand, and hauled out the garbage bag with the other.

"Come on." I grabbed Chelsea's arm and dragged her across the concourse. There was no time to lose.

"Hi there, can I talk to you for a minute?" I called out to the janitor. He was just about to tie a knot in the garbage bag and set it on his cart. He looked like he was Mark Clark's age, mid-twenties. He was tall and straight up and down skinny, with a wispy brown mustache and sad eyes. Over his pocket there was a name patch that said LEO.

He opened his mouth to speak, but before he could say anything, I started talking. That's something I've learned. When in doubt, be friendly and start talking. Most people are too polite to just turn on their heel, and while the words are pouring out of your mouth you can think of what you want to say. "Leo, my friend here lost her passport. She thinks she might have thrown it away by accident when she was getting coffee."

I could feel Chelsea's big blue eyes sending rays of pure exasperation into the back of my head. Of course Chelsea wasn't the type of person to lose her passport— she probably had a designer passport holder that matched her designer suitcase—but I needed to make it sound important so Leo would help us.

Leo let out a huge sigh and dropped the bag. "Knock yourselves out, ladies."

"I really like your sunglasses," I said.

I took the bag from him and dragged it over to one of the small metal tables lined up outside the shop. I flashed him a big grin as I sat down and opened the bag. Leo frowned a little, as if he couldn't tell whether I was goofing with him or not.

"We'll try to make it quick," I added.

He shrugged and looked away, as if we were doing something too personal to watch.

Chelsea sat down in the small metal chair opposite me, muttering under her breath. I hauled another chair around so the bag was between us. I pulled out the empty paper cups and stacked them on the table. Chelsea pulled out every lipstick-stained napkin and plastic cup lid with the tips of her fingers, as though the cooties were going to race up her arm, into her ears, and straight into her brain. I know I know I know: It *was* disgusting, but it could have been worse. We could be going through a giant landfill in some tropical country on the hottest day of the year. Or hey, cleaning out the fridge at my house.

"We don't have all day," I whispered. "We've got to pick this up." I plunged my arm deeper into the bag. I pulled out every smooth slip of paper I could get my hands on and stuffed it into my pocket. People stared at us as they passed, wondering what in the heck we were doing. "Lose something?" snickered one teenaged girl. "A contact lens? Your mind?" Her friends snorted with hilarity.

"You're sure it was around ten thirty?" I asked.

"Didn't I already say that about a thousand times?"

"Look, if you want my help, don't act all stuck-up, all right?"

Chelsea sulked, but dug her arm into the garbage bag.

"Any luck?" said Leo the janitor. He kept glancing over at us, tugging on one end of his mustache, suspicious. "I gotta keep moving here."

Then, down near the bottom, I pinched a long slip that had curled around a damp cup, hauled it up along with a few other crumbled bags and grease-spotted paper plates, glanced at it quickly.

She shoots, she scores. I was sure this was it. I leaped up, knocking my chair over.

"Gosh darn," I said, trying to sound convincing. "It's not here. But thanks anyway." I stuffed all the empty latte cups, napkins, old newspapers, half-eaten muffins, and all the rest of the trash back into the bag.

"I guess you can probably get it replaced," the janitor said to Chelsea.

"I—" Chelsea began. I could tell that for a second she'd forgotten the lie about the passport. I grabbed her arm and dragged her down the concourse, toward the escalator.

"We're golden," I said. I had the name of the lady who'd bought Chelsea's ring. I felt like running, or skipping, actually. I hadn't really thought this idea would work, but it was the only thing I could think of. I could hear Chelsea's flip-flops slapping against her feet as she scampered along.

"Let's see it!" she said.

"Wait until we get downstairs," I said, hopping on the escalator. I hate the down escalator almost as much as I hate birds; the long sinister-looking metal steps always look as if they're disappearing into nothing, that stepping onto them is stepping over a cliff.

I wouldn't look at the slip until we were on the MAX

speeding back toward Portland. There was a bunch of writing on it, stuff that we couldn't make any sense of, then this: Dbl T Car Sy XX Fmy Latte.

Chelsea grabbed it out of my hand. She had no trouble deciphering the code. "Double Tall Caramel Soy Extra-Foamy Latte. That's it. I'm positive. I remember thinking, *What's with the extra foamy business? Aren't lattes already like half foam?*"

The time stamped on it was 10:27, and the name on it was Sylvia Soto.

- 3 -

She totally looked like a Sylvia. I'm sure that's her," said Chelsea. She kept clapping her hands together. "This really kicks serious willy."

"Kicks serious *willy*?" I snorted with laughter.

"They say it all the time in London, all right?"

Finding the receipt with Sylvia's name on it may have kicked serious willy, but by the time we arrived at the MAX stop near Chelsea's house, I'd run out of ideas. We had Sylvia Soto's name, but now what? The sun was still a gray ball behind the clouds. I retied my hair in a knot on top of my head. Chelsea could barely sit still. She kept wishing aloud for some hand sanitizer. She wanted to go home and change her clothes.

Since I couldn't think of anything better to do, I said that sounded like a good idea. I figured we could use

Chelsea's computer to Google Sylvia Soto. That would probably be the best way to find her.

Casa Clark was big and old, but Chelsea's house was really big and really old. It was the dictionary definition of rich. Look it up and there you will see the big brick porch, the white pillars, and dark green door. It looked as if a president of something might live there. Her street was wide, with ancient trees shading the sidewalk.

Inside Chelsea's house it smelled like lemon and ammonia. Everything was matchy matchy. The two white sofas in the living room matched each other, and the coffee table and the end tables all matched. Even though there were genuine paintings on the walls—close-ups of the insides of different flowers—they also seemed to match.

You could tell that this was not a house where someone said "Hey, look at this cool poster of the Ramones" or whatever, and stuck it on the wall just because it was fun to look at. Maybe that's the difference between having a mom on the premises full-time and living in a house run by boys. Chelsea de Guzman did not have a life-size cardboard James Bond in his tuxedo in her entryway, like we did.

No one was home except the housekeeper, who was in the kitchen . . . doing guess what? . . . cleaning out the refrigerator. Chelsea introduced us.

"Minerva, Agata. Agata, Minerva. Do we have any

hand sanitizer?" Chelsea motioned washing her hands, and Agata nodded toward the corner of the kitchen sink. The kitchen was all white with a huge stainless steel refrigerator and stove. It looked both plain and fancy at the same time. It reminded me of a laboratory. There were no magnets of creepy critters on the fridge.

"Where are Louis and Jeanette?" asked Chelsea, squirting a worm of the clear sanitizer gel into her narrow palms. At the Clark house, we would have just turned on the tap, run our hands beneath whatever temperature water came out, and called it clean. I knew Louis was Mr. de Guzman and I assumed Jeanette was Chelsea's mom.

Agata shrugged. "Not here," she said. Agata was about a foot shorter than me and from a foreign land. She didn't wear a housekeeper uniform, like you see in the movies, but a long-sleeved white blouse and black slacks. I didn't recognize her accent. She was cleaning a bottle of soy sauce with a towel and Windex, as if it was a window that everybody had to look through all the time.

"Excellent," said Chelsea, sighing and suddenly relaxed, as though our problems were automatically solved, just because her parents weren't around.

I thought Chelsea would take me up to her room. I know if she came to my house I would have taken her up to my room, but instead she led me to another matchy room, with rows of bookcases and a flat-screen TV and white shag carpeting and more white sofas. This was the equivalent of our TV room, I guessed, where the only available place to sit was Cat Pee Couch, or else the leaking blue beanbag chair.

"You can use that computer." She waved her hand toward a small wooden desk in the corner, a flat-screen monitor and sleek keyboard positioned in the center. Even Mark Clark, whose business was computers, didn't have such a nice setup.

She left me there while she went to change. I could hear her flip-flops slapping up first one flight of stairs, then another, then another. From the kitchen I could hear Agata singing.

The computer was already on. I Googled Sylvia Soto and found an accountant in Orlando, a psychologist in Buena Park, California, and a social worker in El Paso. I didn't think any of these were our Sylvia Soto. Our Sylvia didn't sound much older than my brothers, and certainly not old enough to be a psychologist or those other jobs. Nor did whitepages.com have anyone resembling Sylvia Soto. For $9.95 one company would do a background search, but you needed a credit card, which I didn't have. Just as I was thinking Chelsea might have one, there was a sudden ferocious scrabbling sound.

The instant I recognized it as dog toenails scrabbling across wood floors, a pair of ginger and white corgis with pointed ears and foxy faces roared into the room, leaping over the arms of the white sofa, wrestling and nipping at each other's heels. I could see why people say that corgis are big dogs in little-dog bodies.

"Hey hey HEY!" said Chelsea, clapping her hands to try to get them off the couch. She'd changed into a new small skirt and long-sleeved T-shirt. "Get off the couch. Bad dogs! Agata, where's Frank?"

Silence from the kitchen.

Chelsea sat on the couch and the two dogs piled on top of her, each trying to find the best spot on her lap from which to lick her neck. They were hilarious, funnier even than Jupiter, and if you know anything about ferrets, you'll know that for pure funniness, ferrets are about the funniest creatures around.

"Agata!" Chelsea sighed and shoved the dogs onto the floor. They scrambled right back up.

From the other room, yet another one appeared. He had more white on his coat than the others. He trotted over to me, turned, and sat down with his back facing me, the better to give him a good pet.

"Is this Frank?" I asked. I reached down and scratched him behind his ears.

Chelsea let out a sharp laugh. I recognized it as the same laugh that used to come out of her when she and the other Chelsea in our class (the lactose-intolerant Chelsea, not this one), used to make fun of me. I reached down to pet the dog-that-was-not-Frank. I scratched him behind the ears. Every time I stopped, he backed himself up until he was sitting on my foot.

"Frank is our dog sitter. Really, he's more of like our dog nanny, except unlike a real nanny he only works about an hour in the morning and an hour at night. Winkin' and Blinkin' are champion show dogs. Their sire even won second place at the Westminster Dog Show one year. They need exercise and special care and stuff. That's Ned you've got over there. He's kind of a loser dog, not at all up to the breed standard. Doesn't have enough orange in his coat, or something. You'd have to ask my mom. She's a total freak over these dumb dogs. Did you find the phone number?"

"Nope." I told her about needing a credit card for the background search. I patted my lap and Ned jumped right up. I didn't think he was a loser dog at all. I thought he was totally adorable.

"Well, now what?" Chelsea kicked her flip-flops off and stuck her tan legs out in front of her. "Do you like this color on my toes? It's called Suzy Sells Sushi by the Seashore. Do you think it's too lavenderish? We should go get a pedicure. Have you ever had a pedicure?"

"I thought you were so afraid of your dad grounding you off the computer that you'd do anything to get the ring back."

"I am," she said. "It's just . . . he only takes it away for a day or two. Then my mom tells him he's being a

37

control freak and they have one of those whispered ar-
guments and we all wind up going out and getting Thai
food. You know how it is."

No, I did not know how it was. I took the receipt out
of my pocket again and read it from top to bottom.

"Maybe we can call the credit card company and pretend we're Sylvia. The last four numbers of her card are
on here," I said.

"And then what do we do—ask for our own address?"

She had a point. "We could say we're calling to make
sure they had our new address, and ask them to read the
old one back to us."

"We could. But won't we have to tell them the whole
number? Not just the last four?"

"Yeah. Probably." Whenever I heard my dad on the
phone complaining about some bill, he was always rat-
tling off a million numbers. "Do you guys have a phone
book?"

"If you can't find her name on the Internet, it's not
going to be in the phone book," snorted Chelsea. But
she pulled herself off the couch and pulled open a few
cupboards beneath one of the bookcases. Winkin' and
Blinkin' lunged after her, nipping at her bare heels. Ned
stayed on my lap, as if he knew he couldn't compete.
Poor Ned. He was such a sweetie. He did have a big
ginger-colored blotch on his shoulder, but I guess that
wasn't enough. I poked my nose into his neck fur. I love

the smell of dog. I've never had a dog. Jupiter was supposed to be a test run; if I could take care of him, then maybe my parents would consider a dog. But then they got a divorce, and everyone forgot about it.

Chelsea found the White Pages, sat down on the edge of the chair at the desk, and tucked her hair behind her ears. I watched her as she paged through. I could see why the boys thought she was one of the cutest girls in our class. She *was* cute, in that kind of regular way, straight dark blond hair parted in the middle, blue eyes, pug nose, small white teeth, and a pointed chin. Totally breed standard, like Winkin' and Blinkin'. I was more like Ned. Which is how I liked it.

"Hey!" She stood straight up. "Here's a Sylvia Soto on SE Albertine Crest. Apartment 1E. Do you think it's her?"

"Only one way to find out," I said, standing up and setting Ned on the floor. He sat at my feet again, wagging the little stump he had instead of a tail.

Back down to the MAX station we went. Really, it was only six long blocks away. Still, Chelsea complained as if we were slashing our way through an equatorial jungle in the wrong shoes. My new friend was turning out to be the dictionary definition of moody: Look it up in the dictionary and there you will find her pouty face. I am moody; all we middle school girls are, but she'd already sped through about six moods since she'd called earlier in the afternoon.

The second we boarded the light rail she said, "What IS it with this dumb train? It reeks in here. I can't believe I'm doing this." She pinched her nose between two fingers, glared at the lady with the thick glasses across the aisle who was reading a small black Bible.

"How else are we supposed to get to Sylvia Soto's place?" I asked. "You got any spare jetpacks laying around maybe?"

"There's no need to be snotty, Minerva."

I reached across her and pressed the plastic strip that ran under the window to request the next stop.

"Eeow. Do you know how many people have touched that thing?" She pulled a tiny bottle of hand sanitizer from her purse, squirted some in my hand. "I don't know why we couldn't have just called her."

"We tried to call her. About ten times. Here, look, let's try it again." I reached in my front pocket for my Bluetooth—the tiny wireless earpiece that came with my new phone. I clipped it over the back of my ear. We probably won't get flying cars in my lifetime, but my Bluetooth was almost as good. It fit in the palm of my hand. I pressed the small button in the center of the device and it redialed Sylvia's number. I sat there with my arms folded across my chest, wagging my foot, pretend humming, dum-de-dum-dum, while I waited for my call to go to voice mail, as I knew it would. "Gosh, no one home, who'd believe it?"

"All right, all right," said Chelsea.

"You said you needed to get your ring back before your dad got home and that's what we're doing," I said.

"I know," she sighed. "I just don't think I'm cut out for all this detective stuff."

"It's better than sitting around doing nothing," I said. "That ring is now worth millions, you said so yourself."

"But I like doing nothing," said Chelsea. "Doing nothing is good for your soul."

I snorted.

Sylvia Soto lived in a small dingy pink apartment building that just about matched Chelsea's pinky-lavender nail polish. It was only two stories, and the front doors all opened out onto a wide alley. The back faced a used furniture store on a busy street. It wouldn't have looked so sad in California maybe, or Florida, with a swimming pool and some bright golden sunlight shining down. As it was, it faced the Dumpsters, which were propped open with bags of rotten garbage.

Sylvia's apartment was on the end. A cherry red mountain bike was chained to the railing by the front door. At the other end two little boys played with their Matchbox cars; their mother sat in a dining room chair behind the apartment's screen door and watched them, while also watching the big TV on the other side of her small living room.

I knocked on Sylvia Soto's front door. From inside we could hear the electronic machine gun sounds of a video game. A dog started barking without much authority. The machine gun noises stopped and a boy pulled open the door.

He was one of those boys who was probably our age, but looked as if he'd been shaving for years. He was my height—five eight, give or take—and had chocolate brown hair that hung in his eyes, high cheekbones, and red lips. I could feel Chelsea beside me, taking in all of his fine qualities. In his arms, he was holding a black pug, who you could tell was glad for the company. He worked his little black nose like mad, trying to catch our scent.

"Yeah?" said the boy.

"Is Sylvia around?" I asked.

"Who wants to know?" he said.

I know we were two strange girls who showed up on his doorstep, but even so, his response seemed harsh.

"Well . . . we do!" giggled Chelsea. "Yup, we do." She flipped her hair over her shoulder. Suddenly, she'd turned into a total flirt monster. "What's your name, you cutie-wootie, you wuffin pupplet, you doggin woggins." She pursed her lips and cooed like a lunatic, tickling the pug under his chin. He ogled her with glee. His eyes were so far apart he looked like a very cuddly fish.

"I didn't know they had black pugs," she said. "Did you get him from a breeder?"

"No, the pound."

The pug was in heaven, but the boy just stood there staring at us, stone-faced. That's the thing about flirt monster mode—you never know when it's not going to work, and you wind up looking like you need to be on medication. Finally he said, "Who are you?"

"When do you expect her back?" I asked quickly. I didn't want to get into who we were.

"How do you know my sister?" he said.

"Eeps!" said Chelsea. "Oh, this sucks!"

The boy and I both looked over at Chelsea at the same time. She'd bent her head, had her finger against her eyelid. "I hate it when this happens. My contact floats up under my eyelid." She looked up, blinked, and moved her eyeballs up to the left. "Can you see it?" she asked me.

I didn't even know Chelsea wore contacts. I leaned close, pretended to peer into her blue eyes.

"I don't see anything," I said, quite truthfully.

"Do you have a mirror? Argh. I hate this." She opened her tiny green leather bag, pawed around inside. "Do you—I know this is a huge favor—could I use your bathroom mirror, do you think?"

I could tell the boy didn't know quite what to make of the situation. His dark eyes shifted from Chelsea to me, and back to Chelsea. At that moment, in the apartment behind him, a cell phone rang. The boy exhaled, frustrated. "Sure, come in. It's around the corner, there."

The door made a scraping sound as it passed over the gold shag carpet. The place smelled like cooking, and only a little like dog.

He grabbed the phone eagerly, then seemed disappointed at the identity of the caller. "Yeah . . . sure. . . . All right. . . . On the set by six a.m. . . . Right." He hung up. He seemed even gloomier than when he answered the door.

As I walked past him, I stopped and examined the image paused on the television screen, some blue and silver robotic-looking guy with an enormous weapon that looked like a cross between a dolphin and a chain saw. "You playing Halo 2? I love Halo 2."

"It's all right," he said. He set the black pug on the blue couch, then thrust his hands deep in the pockets of his cargo pants. I pegged him as one of those impossibly cute boys who was also impossibly shy and therefore, plain old impossible.

Chelsea dutifully scooted around the corner and into the bathroom, where she made a bunch of searching-for-her-contact-behind-her-eyelid ahhhs, ummms, and ughhhhs. She talked a little too much about why she'd decided to get contacts and give up wearing glasses.

I stood in front of the set, chatting about Halo 2,

which I didn't love, which I thought was pretty lame, like a lot of first-person shooter video games, but which my brothers liked to play.

It was a tiny apartment without much in it. I guessed they had either just moved in, or else they didn't have much money to spend on decorating. You could see most of the apartment from the living room; the blue couch took up one side of the wall, the big TV took up most of the other.

There was nothing on the walls except a poster of Puerto Vallarta, Mexico—a tiny town of red roofs and pink flowers tumbling into the blue ocean—and a calendar tacked over the television. I stepped closer. It was from the Portland Humane Society. The picture for June showed three gray kitties peering out from inside a wicker basket. For the last half of the month there was the same note every day: "Tonio—Shooting" and then a time, usually 7:00 or 8:00 A.M.

Shooting what? Shooting practice? Tonio was probably the boy, but what was shooting? Maybe he was in a summer basketball league?

A bookshelf of phony wood stood against the far wall. A single row of fat paperbacks, and in front of them, a collection of glass unicorns. The other shelves held stacks of folded clothes, T-shirts, jeans, and camo pants—obviously the bookcase did double duty as the boy's dresser drawers.

45

A few steps from the bookshelf, beneath a window that looked out into the alley, there was a wooden table. I guessed it was where they ate. It was bare, except for a bunch of yellow daisies stuck in a jelly jar running low on water, and a pile of unopened mail. Sitting beside the jelly jar was something small and silver. The ring?

"Oh cool," I said. "I love daisies. They're my favorite flowers!"

I walked to the table, picked up the jelly jar, and pretended to smell the small yellow flowers. Of course, they don't smell like anything, and I looked like sort of an idiot, but I could see out of the corner of my eye that the ring on the table was Chelsea's. I put the flowers back on the table. "These need some water," I said, just for something to say.

Moments earlier Chelsea had finished her fake contact lens adjustment in front of the bathroom mirror and joined us in the living room, where she'd starting asking the boy about Puerto Vallarta. Had he ever been there? Oh, he was from there? How cool!

She must have glimpsed the ring on the table only seconds after I did, for she was at my shoulder in a flash. The black pug jumped off the couch and barked at her twice. He hopped up and down, as if playtime was about to begin.

For all her tiresome girly-girly business, Chelsea was quick. She played point guard for our basketball team and ran track. She snatched up the ring, took one hard look at it, set it back on the table, and walked back out of the apartment, her face blank as a zombie. I looked down. The center stone was missing.

"Thanks," I said to him, hurrying after Chelsea. "I love your dog."

He stared at me for a second, but was mostly occupied with trying to keep the pug from running out after us. The expression on his face was clear: *What's going on here?* But I could tell he was having a hard time putting it together.

Outside, I caught up with Chelsea. She marched down the sidewalk back toward the bus stop, sobbing. The dull clouds had gotten bored and started spitting on us, typical early summer drizzle. "Oh my God I am *so* dead. I am *so* dead. *I am so dead!*" She stopped. "I'm going to throw up."

And then poor Chelsea did throw up, right there in the shrubbery outside Starbucks. I held her hair back. I felt terrible for her, but kept getting sidetracked: Now, this was a real mystery. The girl named Sylvia Soto had the now-worthless ring, but who had the red diamond?

- 4 -

Here's a question: Why is it that the trip back always seems shorter than the trip there? It took no time at all to get back to Chelsea's. It started raining for real, small pestering drops. I didn't ask her any more questions about the ring, and she didn't complain about the germs of public transportation.

My thoughts were a swarm of bees caught in a jar. I wondered about so many things. First, was it a complete coincidence that Sylvia Soto bought the ring off Chelsea, just like that? It was impossible, right? And why would someone like Mr. de Guzman transport a ring into the country that way? I had to admit, when Chelsea had told me he'd switched the red cut-glass stone out for a real gem, I thought she might have been making it up. Chelsea was, after all, a drama queen known to lie on occasion. Was this something jewelers did all the time and people just didn't know about it? And what system was Mr. de Guzman trying to beat, anyway?

We walked part of the way from the MAX station together in the rain. Neither of us said a thing, then Chelsea said, "I really hate throwing up."

"Yeah, I know," I said.

When we reached the corner where I had to turn up to go home, I told her I'd call her if I thought of anything, and she said she'd let me know what her dad had found out. Since he thought she'd lost the ring, he probably already had airport security and the FBI and Spider-Man turning the city upside down looking for it.

I let myself in the back door with my key. At Casa Clark there are two back doors, one that goes from the backyard to the kitchen and one that goes from the driveway into the back hallway. This is the one everyone uses, unless they are taking out the garbage. The computer room is just off the back hallway. As I hurried past I could hear the sounds of cartoon monsters yelping in pain. I leaned into the room and spied the back of Mark Clark. He sat on the edge of his chair in his business-casual khaki pants and a blue polo shirt playing EverQuest, his all-time favorite video game. He was battling a gang of killer mermaids. Morgan was probably in his room reading. From the basement came the sound of the same three notes on a bass guitar—Quills practicing. This was just how I liked it: all the brothers home, but too busy to ask me all those boring adult questions that make you want to pull out your eyebrows like, "How was your day?"

"Hi, I'm home!" I called out to anyone who might have been listening. I took the stairs two at a time. If I hung around downstairs Mark Clark would soon finish fighting his mermaids and feel the need to debrief about my cleaning the fridge, which I didn't think I could stand. I had so much to think about.

I needed an IP with my best friend Reggie, but I doubted I was going to get one. An IP was Reggie/Minerva code for an In Person, talking face-to-face. Reggie was the smartest boy I knew. He had at his fingertips many facts about black holes, hieroglyphics, and those people who spend all their free time re-creating the Civil War. I have known him since our moms took a water aerobics class together when they were pregnant with us, then pushed us in our strollers together in the park. Reggie got straight A's, except in Citizenship, because he was always blurting out the answers without raising his hand or putting fake severed fingers in people's desks. Last year our seventh-grade teacher, Mrs. Dayton-Bunnsted, called Reggie a True Test from God. We go to a Catholic school, even though we aren't Catholic, because Catholics offer a superior education, which as far as I can see means they care about spelling.

I used to be able to get IPs with Reggie any time I wanted, even after dark on a school night. We would drop everything for each other. But that was before he fell in drooling stupid love with Amanda Crossley, aka Amanda the Panda.

Amanda the Panda was Reggie's girlfriend. And I don't mean girl-space-friend, I mean girlfriend, one word, as in they hold hands when no one's around and kiss and other things I can't bear to think about.

This isn't because I have a thing for Reggie. As you know, I have a thing for Kevin, who was coming home from fly-fishing in Montana in 164 hours, give or take. I would love to have an IP with Kevin, but I'm not sure I can talk to him about the same kind of things I talk to Reggie about. I am a little afraid to find out that maybe Kevin, who is my almost-boyfriend, is not as smart as Reggie, who is my best friend-even-though-he-is-a-boy. If it is true, that Kevin isn't smart like Reggie, what does it mean? That I should be with Reggie? Or is it okay to be with a boy who is not the smartest boy you know? It is so confusing sometimes.

I do not have a thing for Reggie. At all, at all, at *all.* It's just Amanda the Panda—Amanda Crossley, who's one year younger than us, and wears too much black mascara that runs when she cries, and she is always crying, because she is a ballet dancer and a Sensitive Soul—is totally annoying. Amanda the Panda has been a ballet dancer since she was three years old. Every year for the talent show, between some third grader messing up a magic trick and a trio of fifth graders lip-syncing "Grease," there's Amanda the Panda in her ballet costume, with pink tights and a pink tutu, performing some ultra-arty, ultra-embarrassing dance to some excruciating *musique classique,* her thin no-color hair pulled back in a bun so tight it looks as if one sudden move is going to squeeze her eyeballs out of her head and into the row of kindergarteners sitting cross-legged in the front.

And now Reggie, who is so smart in every other way you can think of, is crushing madly on her, and spends every waking moment either at Amanda the Panda's house, or on the phone talking to her, or on his computer IMing her. Quills is writing a song for Humongous Bag of Cashews called "The Mystery of Love and Attraction," and I think it's about just this type of human weirdness. At least crushing on Kevin makes sense. He is totally hot and nice and is into origami the same way I'm into rebuses and is taking Japanese next year in high school.

As I sat down in front of my computer to instant message Reg I had a strange thought: What if people wondered why Kevin was crushing on *me*? What if to all Kevin's friends, I was like *his* Amanda the Panda? What if they had a nickname for me?

I ran my hands down my face, shoved that thought

straight out of my head. No wonder there were all those songs about how love made you insane.

I could see that Reggie was logged on; his screen name, BorntobeBored, was the first one on my Buddy List, under the Group "Annoying Freak." LOL. He was the only one in that group.

Ferretluver: Knock knock

While I waited, I flipped through my rebus notebook. I used to write rebuses all the time to occupy myself, but I hadn't done one in a long time. I flipped back to the beginning of the notebook and read my early rebuses, all written with sparkling gel pens. My first one was: HIGH HIGH. Too high. I remember having written that in the fifth grade and thinking I would someday get my notebook published. I felt sad and embarrassed all at once, thinking back on those earnest hopes. I didn't allow the thought to go any further: that one day I would be looking back at these days and feeling the same.

Reggie didn't respond, so I started harassing him.

Ferretluver: Who's there?
Ferretluver: Justin
Ferretluver: Justin who?
Ferretluver: Justin the neighborhood and thought I'd say hello! REGGIE! ARE U THERE?
BorntobeBored: Knock knock

Ferretluver: Where were you?

BorntobeBored: You're supposed to say "who's there?"

Ferretluver: LOL

BorntobeBored: Why r you laffing? I haven't even gotten to the punch line.

Ferretluver: What do you know about red diamonds, and transporting them into the United States from London?

BorntobeBored: "Ring"

At that second my cell phone rang. I popped my Bluetooth onto my ear and pressed the little button.

"So what do you know about diamonds?" I asked.

"Besides that most of them are over three billion years old, or two-thirds the age of the planet?"

"What else? What about red diamonds?"

"Red diamonds? Very rare . . ." His voice trailed off. I could hear the telltale sound of computer keys tapping: He was IMing someone, probably The Panda.

"Reg?"

"Diamonds are the hardest objects on earth. Made of pure carbon. The only thing that can cut a diamond is another diamond. The word diamond comes from the Greek *adamas.* Means invincible." He rattled this off as he typed.

"We were talking about red diamonds."

"Right . . ." *Tap tap tap tap tap tap tap.*

"Are you IMing Amanda the Panda?"

"Do you have to call her that? She has nothing but nice things to say about you."

"Yeah, right."

"Why do you need to know about . . ." *Tap tap tap tap tap.* ". . . red diamonds?"

"Call me when you can actually talk, would you?"

"Mandy says hey," he said.

"Gackarffaguga," I said. I am the *queen* of choking noises. They sound so authentic I better not start choking for real because no one who knows me would ever save me. "*Listen* to yourself, Reg."

"Listen, dude, she's really nice," he said lamely.

"Whatever." I hung up. The truth is, I was totally jealous, even though I don't like Reggie and am madly in crush with Kevin. Put that in your song, Quills.

I guess it was just me and Google. I typed in "red diamonds" and learned that diamonds come in every color of the rainbow, but the colored ones are freaks of nature. Colored diamonds are called fancy diamonds and usually only special fancy diamond collectors are interested in them. The most common fancy diamonds are yellow, pink, blue, and a sparkling brown known as champagne diamonds. The coloration is caused by other elements mixed with the carbon. Boron causes blue diamonds. Nitrogen causes yellow diamonds. Red diamonds are rare and expensive. They come from a mine called the Argyle Mine in Australia.

Diamonds are measured in carats, which I always thought were carrots. When Mark Clark was engaged briefly to Lulu he bought her a one-carat ring. It was no bigger than a pea. Still, it cost a lot of money.

It seemed as if the biggest, most famous diamonds were cursed. The Black Orlov diamond is as big as a walnut, and was stolen from the forehead of an idol in India by a monk. Everyone who owned it after that committed suicide, including two Russian princesses. The Hope diamond is a famous violet-blue diamond that was also stolen from the forehead of an idol in India. It was cursed, too. The Frenchman who stole it was torn apart by wild dogs. Now I was really getting the creeps. Then Louis XVI somehow got a hold of it and gave it to his queen, Marie Antoinette, and they were both beheaded. The Hope diamond was sold again and again, and everyone who owned it suffered terrible luck because of it.

I wondered if Mr. de Guzman's diamond was cursed. It was much smaller than the Black Orlov diamond and the Hope diamond, so probably it was just a face-in-the-crowd diamond, no big deal other than its strange rare color.

It was nearly dark outside, but there were no stars. The only light in my room was the blue glare from my computer monitor. I really hoped Mr. de Guzman hadn't stolen his red diamond from the head of an Indian idol, or from anyone else, for that matter. I suddenly didn't like being all alone in my room on the third floor, and was relieved when Mark Clark called me down to dinner.

My brothers were already seated at the big dining room table. Since our mom left and our dad is always away on business, Mark Clark has come to believe it's his duty to have a sit-down dinner a few times a week, and no one complains, even though we always ate too late.

I sat down at my place and dug into my chicken enchiladas without saying a word. My mind was going round and round. No one said anything, other than Morgan, who asked someone to pass the salad.

"This summer isn't going to be this way," said Mark Clark, out of the blue.

I looked up. What was he talking about? "What way?" I asked.

"If you don't find something to do, I will find something for you to do. You're not going to spend the entire three months on the computer."

What *was* he talking about? I'd been running around like a mad person all day. I'd already taken MAX to the airport and I'd seen the inside of Chelsea de Guzman's fancy house, and met Winkin', Blinkin', and Ned, her champion show dog corgis—well, except for the adorable Ned, who was worth ten of the other two dogs, in my humble opinion. I'd been busy. Of course, Mark Clark didn't know that, and I wasn't about to tell him. "I cleaned the refrigerator," I said.

"And then what? You went over and hung out at a friend's house, then came home and spent the last few hours IMing."

"Sor-ry," I said. "I thought it was called summer *vacation* for a reason."

"Lose the tone. Now."

"Sorry." I dropped my fork on my plate and folded my hands in my lap. I wore a pair of baggy blue jean shorts. If I had any scabs on my knees, I'd have been fiddling with them, but mostly we modern children do not have many scabs. We are the Knee and Elbow Pad Generation.

"I'm serious, Minerva. You cannot lie around all summer IMing your friends."

"I am not lying around IMing my friends. That's actually impossible anyway. I have to sit at my desk to IM my friends."

Quills snorted. "She got you there," he said. Quills drank his entire glass of milk straight down. He loves to make trouble, just because.

I didn't know where this conversation was going, but my Spidey sense was telling me it wasn't good. My enchiladas were getting cold. Plus, the fact was, once Kevin got home, I was planning on IMing him every possible minute I could.

"I've gone ahead and signed you up for a class at Kid-academy," said Mark Clark.

"What kind of a class?" I asked. I couldn't believe these words were coming out of the mouth of my most cool brother. He signed me up for a *class*. In *summer*. Mark Clark didn't play bass guitar in a rock band like Quills, nor was he a junk food vegetarian college student and philosopher like Morgan, but nestled deep inside Mark Clark, next to the nerd and ultra-responsible almost-dad, was the person who truly remembered what it was like to be my age.

"What class!" I squawked.

"You might enjoy it," said Morgan, who had been quiet during the entire meal. He was wearing his orange and black ear flap hat and eating the radishes out of his salad. He was always in favor of taking some dweeby class.

"How do you know?"

"I said you might," said Morgan. "There's no law that says that your brain has to shut down for the summer."

"I've signed you up for basic electronics," said Mark Clark. "Have an open mind."

"Basic electronics! *Basic electronics!*" Having an open mind was exactly what I was not going to do. I intended keeping it shut as tight as an unopened pickle jar. I was mad. My scalp was getting all hot underneath my hair.

I wasn't sure what you might learn in a basic electronics class, but it sounded too geeky, even for me. And I am a geek. I have a ferret named Jupiter. I collect rebuses. I don't care too much about clothes or makeup. (Although I don't mind a little dark blue eyeliner now and again. I also have been known to paint my toenails.)

I put my hands together and begged Mark Clark. I whined like I'm not supposed to. I could smell the spicy bad body odor of the boys in the class already, see their smeary glasses and mossy teeth.

"Please," I said. "I am not going to lie around all summer IMing. I promise. Most of my friends won't be around to IM anyway. They're going to summer school and stuff. I'll sign up for the library read-a-thon program. I'll . . . I'll eat broccoli for every meal. I'll take out the garbage without being asked. Please." The more I begged, the more frantic I got.

Mark Clark carefully cut his enchilada with the side of his fork. He shoveled up a bite and placed it in his mouth. He chewed slowly. I could tell there was no way I was going to get out of this. "It won't kill you. And I think you might—"

"Dude, do *not* say 'get a charge out of it,' " said Quills.

Mark Clark shrugged and kept eating without looking up.

"All right. When is it?" I asked, pushing away my plate. I'd hardly eaten anything.

"Saturday mornings. It won't kill you." Mark Clark didn't tell me to eat my enchiladas, which prevented me from totally despising him.

"Tomorrow's Saturday," I said.

"It's from nine to noon," he said. "Downtown."

I sighed long and loud and slumped in my chair. It wasn't as if I had any big ideas about how to find Chelsea's missing red diamond, but now I would have to waste my morning learning about switches and circuits and whatever.

"There's something else," said Mark Clark.

"What?" I said. What could it be? Some new and awful chore?

"It's no big deal," he said. "Mom's coming home."

"Just for MC's birthday," Quills added quickly. Even though we were all technically MCs in our house— Quills's real name was Michael—MC was what we called Mark Clark.

I must have had a weird look on my face, because Mark Clark added, "Not for good. She's not moving back or anything. Just visiting for a few days."

I didn't know what to think. I took a sip of milk just for something to do. It was nonfat. Yuck yuck *yuck*. There were other kids in our class whose parents were divorced, but I was the only kid who didn't live with her mom. We all said we wanted Mom to be happy, but we said it too much. We said it all the time. Once, I overheard Morgan and Quills talking about how sucky it was that she'd left while I was still such a kid. It was better to hate them for saying that than to hate her for leaving. I didn't like being called a kid, is what I told myself.

"May I be excused to start the dishes?" When I added this part about the dishes the brothers never said I had to sit and wait until everyone was finished eating. I needed to get away and think.

I took my time unloading the clean dishes from the dishwasher. I made extra sure to put them away with care. Every dinner plate had a chip on the edge from when I hurried, which was most of the time. I had a stomachache, but not from the chicken enchiladas. It was as if someone was inside of me sitting on my guts.

Normally I loved it when Mom came home. We went shopping, first for underwear and socks and necessary things, then funny T-shirts (last time I got one that said THERE BETTER BE SOME CHEESE AT THE END OF THIS MAZE), CDs, and silly jewelry. That's how I knew about the cheap rings at Claire's. My mom loved to go there. She said it made her feel festive. I could just see her trying on a charm bracelet and calling across the store to me, "Minnow, come check these out. Aren't they cute?" She was the only one who got away with calling me

Minnow. But I realized I didn't want her to call me Minnow anymore. Since I'd last seen her I'd suffered an electric shock and solved a mystery and had my first kiss and I was nobody's Minnow anymore.

I looked into the window over the sink. Since the time I was tall enough to do the dinner dishes, I loved to look at my reflection. I thought it was magic, that the window turned into a mirror at night. I stared at myself. Maybe that was the reason I needed to help Chelsea solve the mystery of the missing red diamond. Why I *had* to help her. If I solved another good mystery, I would know for sure that the new Minerva was still around, that my confidence hadn't worn off. I felt sure of this. But if Mom came home, I wouldn't be able to slip out and sleuth around. She would want to Do Things Together. All my time would be taken up with bonding.

Plus, there was also the chance that Mom would like the old insecure Minnow better.

I went to my room. I tried to IM Reggie, but he had logged off. I tried to call Reggie, but he wasn't answering. I took out my rebus notebook and wrote ECNALG, backward glance, and felt my spirits lift for the first time since I'd been home.

I went to bed. It was hot in my room. My stomach had a fist in it from not enough dinner and too much worry. Then I did what I always did to make myself go to sleep these days. I remembered the last dance of the year, and dancing with Kevin to "Every Rose Has Its Thorn," which is so lame and sappy, but I didn't care. Even though everyone was sweaty from dancing, he still smelled like soap and chlorine, like all swimmers do. Then I thought about how he kissed me outside in the parking lot before Mark Clark showed up to pick up Hannah and me. It was cold outside, and the wind was coming in off the river. What I tried hard not to think about was that Kevin had been late to the dance, so late that I thought he wasn't going to make it. He apologized as soon as he arrived, said he'd just broken up with his girlfriend and she hadn't taken it very well. I didn't like thinking he'd just had a girlfriend three hours before he was kissing me. He didn't tell me the girlfriend's name, and I didn't ask.

Then, suddenly, it was 8:00 A.M. and the sun was blasting through my curtainless windows. Mark Clark was standing in the doorway telling me it was time to get up. It was already warm in my room. Summer was here, and it seemed, suddenly, as if mine was going to be as cursed as the Hope diamond.

- 5 -

Basic electronics was held downtown in a building near Portland State University, in the middle of a grove of tall glass office buildings and more importantly, half a block from MAX. Mark Clark said he would drop me off, but that I could take MAX home. The day was dark-glasses bright, so different from yesterday it was as if the days of late June weren't even in the same season. I wore a pair of Bermudas, a T-shirt with tiny yellow and pink flowers, and my turquoise Chuck Taylors.

The classroom for basic electronics didn't have any windows. A white board ran along the front, and a name was written on it in big blue letters: Mr. Lawndale. This was obviously the teacher, who was standing at the front of the room behind a long, tall table with a bunch of electronic equipment on it, colorful wires, meters, gauges, and I don't know what all. It looked as if a toaster had exploded up there.

As we wandered in he said, "Find a workbench and sit down, please, please sit down."

Our workbenches were long desks of pale wood that sat three people each. A long, low cubby that held a collection of electronic equipment studded with fancy dials and meters rose up on one side. The classroom filled up slowly.

There were thirteen boys and two girls. The other girl besides me was one of those girls who boys paid attention to, even though if you looked at each of her features they were nothing special. In the Chelsea de Guzman mode, she was skinny and had long dark blond hair, round blue eyes, and a snub nose. She wore extra low-rise jeans and an oversized newsboy hat that engulfed her head. Like most of us, she might as well have been wearing a sign that said: I AM HERE AGAINST MY WILL. She sat down at the workbench in front of me and started text-messaging someone.

The teacher, Mr. Lawndale, wore a red and blue plaid shirt that already had dark sweat rings in the armpits. He was talking to some mom at the front of the room. He had his hand on one hip and kept shoving his glasses up on his nose with the other. The mom was explaining something, and Mr. Lawndale frowned. Then he said, a little too loud: "Look, if your kid doesn't want to be here, I don't want him here either. I don't need it, I simply don't need it!'"

Aren't teachers supposed to be happy and full of love for their profession on the first day of class?

I traded glances with the boy sitting next to me. He must have been having the same sort of thought. He was a little taller than me, with long dark bangs that hung in his eyes and freckles all over his nose. When Mr. Lawndale took roll call, shouting out our first and last names, I learned his name was Bryce Duncan. If I didn't already think Kevin was the cutest boy I knew, I might think that way about Bryce Duncan.

Mr. Lawndale stood behind the exploded toaster table at the front of the room and began with a speech on the importance of learning the fundamentals, but then he went off on resistors and transistors and the ubiquitous NE555 timer integrated circuit and the PIC microcontrollers. He talked about commonplace components, LEDs and switches and batteries. I don't know what he was talking about, but I don't think they were fundamentals, I think they were topics meant to make him look smart and us look dirt-dumb. He had an impatient tone, as if we were all asking one stupid question after the next, even though no one had said a word. The air-conditioning whirred on. I was relieved, because Mr. Lawndale was perspiring like a man about to be found guilty.

"The only way you can possibly *possibly* have a chance at understanding electricity is to think of it as water in a pipe," he said. "Voltage is the water and the amplitude is the water pressure."

My glance wandered over to Bryce Duncan. I noticed he had small moles dotting his arms. He was wearing a black AC/DC T-shirt that had been washed so often it had turned dark gray. I wondered why he was here, whether basic electronics was something he had an interest in, or whether his parents were worried that he would become a juvenile delinquent over the summer unless he had Something To Do.

He reached into his front jeans pocket and fished out a pack of Big Red gum. He looked over just at that moment and saw me watching. "Now longer lasting fresh breath."

"I don't have bad breath!" I said. Mark Clark was an Altoid freak. He ate—and offered—so many Altoids the dentist told him if he didn't lay off he would have fresh breath but no teeth.

Bryce Duncan blushed beneath his freckles. "Naw, I just . . . that's what the stupid ads say."

"Oh, right." I laughed.

The pretty girl, who sat kitty-corner from us, turned around and looked at Bryce Duncan.

Suddenly, I noticed that Mr. Lawndale had fallen silent. He stood at the front of the room with his hands on his hips, glaring around the classroom. At first I thought Bryce Duncan and I were going to get busted for talking, but I looked around the classroom and saw that my classmates were all either stealth text-messaging beneath the desk, or dozing, or fiddling with the electronic equipment. We were one large fifteen-headed organism of Not Paying Attention.

"All right," said Mr. Lawndale. "Fine. I am here to meet your needs, am I not? You need to see what electricity can do, am I right? This is all just boring twaddle, am I right?"

We glanced around. He was being phony nice, that was for sure.

"Take out your breadboards."

Breadboards?

He sighed, reached over into the cubby on the desk nearest the front and pulled out a flat white rectangle the size of a paperback book. Rows of tiny holes ran down each side, with a blank strip in between. Someone asked why they called it a breadboard.

Mr. Lawndale sighed again. "Well, what does it look like to you?"

No one said anything.

"Why, it holds the components," said Mr. Lawndale. "You do know what components are, right? Without our handy breadboards, you'd be forced to wrap the wires around each of the capacitor's legs. How inconvenient is that?"

There was a small storage cabinet on each bench, and from that we were told to find something called a capacitor. It looked like a flattened pencil eraser with two wires sticking out from under it, like legs. Bryce Duncan made his walk around the table a little, as if it was a little alien bug.

Mr. Lawndale then instructed us to plug our capacitor into the breadboard, followed by the red wire and the black wire issuing from the power supply box on our workbench.

"Keep in mind what I said earlier about the important rules of positive and negative electricity," brayed Mr. Lawndale.

Just as I was thinking that maybe basic electronics wasn't so bad, there was the first big snap, followed by another and another. *Crack! Crack!* It was the sound of firecrackers going off, but there were no firecrackers. The sleepiest, most distracted kids jumped, startled. The newsboy hat girl shrieked.

Each and every one of our alien bug capacitors was exploding. They weren't big explosions, but they were loud. The room filled with a strange smell: melted plastic and peanut butter–scented smoke. The moment after the last capacitor blew there was a half second of silence, during which one boy with an Afro said, "Now that rocks."

Mr. Lawndale said, "That rocks? *That rocks?* No, my

friend, that does not rock. That is called an exploding capacitor. That is called a sure way to blow your empty heads clean off. That is called what happens when you're not listening. Did even one of you pay attention to the rules of positive and negative electricity? Was anyone at all listening when I said that you must *always* place the long leg of the capacitor into the positive side of the breadboard, which would be the side with the *red* wire?"

Even though the exploding capacitors were sort of cool, we got the point. The fifteen-headed organism figured that it would be good to pay attention after all, but then irritable Mr. Lawndale, who clearly hated us and needed to find a new career, maybe one in which he does not work with children, threw away his chance at gaining our respect.

He said, "When it comes to electricity, you need to focus or someone will lose an eye."

Then, if Bryce Duncan didn't pipe up: "It's all fun and games until someone loses an eye. Then it's just fun!"

Even though it's an old joke, we started laughing. I felt sorry for Mr. Lawndale, even though he was sort of awful. He had no choice but to stand at the front of the room and push his glasses up on his nose over and over again until we decided to calm down.

The moment class was dismissed I popped on my Bluetooth and phoned Chelsea. Kids streamed out of the building around me into the sunlight. The newsboy hat girl swung off down the street in the direction of Pioneer Place, a fancy downtown mall that Chelsea favors. Bryce Duncan's mom picked him up right out front, in one of those MINI Coopers, red with a black top. I stood on the sidewalk and watched them roar away, waiting for Chelsea to pick up.

"Hey, Minerva," said Chelsea. There was so much noise I could hardly hear her.

"Listen, do you remember whether Sylvia was on the plane with you?"

In the background, I could hear a man's voice and a woman's voice, and the sound of something sliding.

"I didn't see her. But we were in first class, so you don't really see the other people on the plane. They're like all in the back."

"During the flight did your dad mention the diamond?"

"I thought I told you, I didn't know until after we got back that he'd replaced the glass stone with the diamond. It was news to me. So like duh, Minerva."

"No need to go all attitude on me, Chelsea. I was just trying to figure out how Sylvia knew to ask to see the ring. It wasn't just a coincidence, you know?"

"Plus, she was in line ahead of me at Coffee People. How did she know I'd get in line there?"

"Exactly," I said. "So, did you notice her after you

got off the plane? She must have heard you tell your mom you wanted a latte."

"We were in the bathroom when I told my mom I wanted to stop at Coffee People."

"And you said those words? You said, 'Can we stop at Coffee People?' Not like, 'I'd like to get a latte'?"

"No, I said I wanted to stop at Coffee People. We were at the sinks washing our hands. I remember. And there were lots of people around us, people coming in and out. She could have been in there, easily. She could have heard me tell my mom I wanted to go to Coffee People, then gotten a head start and slipped in line before me."

Now we were getting somewhere. I was walking faster and faster, not sure where I was going. I could feel the day warming up, the sun beating down on my head. I passed a store that specialized in clothes from Ireland, then a jewelry store. I stopped and looked into the window at a diamond ring on display. It was just a plain old white diamond, not a rare red one like ours. I felt a twirl of excitement, wondering what would happen next.

I realized Chelsea hadn't said anything for a few seconds, as if she were preoccupied. Through the phone, I could still hear background sounds. I put my finger in my ear so I could hear better. Footsteps on a hard floor. A man with an accent saying, "May I help you, miss?" Then Chelsea said, "I'm looking for a diamond? A red one? Maybe someone brought it in like yesterday?"

The man laughed like Santa. "Ho ho ho! I've never seen a red diamond in all my days, and don't expect to. Did you lose one, miss? Ho ho ho."

"*Chelsea!*" I shrieked into the phone.

"What?" she asked, a trace of annoyance in her voice.

"What are you doing? Where are you?"

"At a pawn shop."

"What are you doing at a pawn shop?"

"I was next door at the nail place getting a pedicure and I thought how a lot of times in movies people pawn stuff, and I thought maybe that Sylvia chick pawned it. I thought I would check it out."

"Sylvia did not pawn it, Chelsea."

"How do you know?"

"Because it's worth a ton of money. Because it wasn't a coincidence that Sylvia just happened to admire your Claire's ring. Somehow, she knew that center stone was valuable."

Then Chelsea must have turned back to the man with the accent, because I heard her say, "If I leave you my number? And anyone comes in with a red diamond could you like call me?"

"A red diamond?" said the man. "You are missing a red diamond?" Even through the phone I could hear new interest in his voice.

"*Chelsea!*"

"*What?!*"

"What are you doing? Don't you know that if Sylvia or someone connected to Sylvia shows up with a red diamond he's just going to keep it?"

"I thought you said she would never pawn it."

"Chelsea, the point is, don't go around blabbing about this. The more people you talk to about this, the more people will be interested in finding it."

I heard a little bell, then the whoosh of a door opening. "You're being a paranoid freak, Minerva."

"This is how you solve a mystery, Chelsea."

"That's right. I forgot. You caught the girl who murdered that bookstore clerk and now you're all Nancy Drew Jr."

"I also cracked that identity theft ring," I said.

"Oh, excuse me. Next you'll have your own TV show."

"Look, do you want me to help you or not?"

"I want you to stop treating me like I'm some kind of an airhead idiot. Jeez."

"I'm sorry," I said. I didn't dare point out that airhead idiot was what they call redundant. It was like saying tuna fish; tuna already *is* a fish.

"I'm just in so much trouble, Minerva! My dad didn't ground me off the computer or anything. He just doesn't look at me or talk to me. And this morning he said the worst thing ever—he said he was *disappointed* in me. It's so much better when they're just mad and being unfair."

"Yeah, I know." There really was nothing worse than when the parents played the I'm-just-so-disappointed-in-you card. "Have you told him we're trying to find it?"

She snorted. "*Right*. He'd think we were so totally lame. He had just about everyone on the planet looking for it at the airport and of course they couldn't find it. This morning he called his insurance guy to see if he could file a claim or something. I feel so terrible."

"Well, I'm going over to Sylvia's again, if you want to meet me," I said.

"What are you going to do there?" asked Chelsea. Her voice sounded flat and depressed.

"I don't know. I'll figure it out when I get there."

The thing was, I felt terrible, too. The ten minutes' worth of fun I'd had sitting next to a cute guy in basic electronics and blowing up the capacitor was over, and now I was facing a mystery I couldn't solve, a friend whose dad was "disappointed" in her, an almost-boyfriend who hadn't called me from Montana like he'd promised, and a visit from my mom that was sure to be totally weird.

- 6 -

When I got to Sylvia's apartment around one o'clock the cherry red mountain bike, which had been chained to the railing the day before, was gone. Many of the apartment doors were open, and from inside I could hear Spanish television, and smell good things cooking, I couldn't begin to name what. Three boys were skateboarding in the parking lot.

As I knocked on Sylvia's door, I watched the boys zooming down a ramp they'd made from an old plywood door propped on a pair of concrete blocks. They stopped for a minute and checked me out. I said hey; they said hey, and I started to think about why boys never seem to outgrow skateboarding but girls do.

I pondered this long after it was clear that no one was home. Then, just as I was about to turn and go, I heard a sound from inside. It sounded like someone dropped a book. I put my ear against the door and listened. I could hear someone moving around. I put my hand on the doorknob and the door eased open a bit.

I felt a pinch of fear in my stomach. Someone was home but didn't want to answer the door. It was one of those great summer days when most people would want to be outside. Some of Sylvia's neighbors had their front doors open to catch the breeze. In addition to the skateboarding boys, a guy was washing his car in the driveway, whistling along to the classic rock station blaring from his radio. It was not a day you would want to be holed up in your apartment. Unless you were a boy who'd stolen a rare red diamond and you thought someone was on to you.

I pushed the door open an inch or so, hoping someone would call out hello or something. Nothing. I stood there another few seconds. I could feel my heart pounding in my eyes. I conjured up something I'd heard once about how being afraid was no excuse not to do something. The question was, of course, was this a smart thing to be doing?

I pushed the door open wider and stepped inside. "Hello?"

I pulled the door closed behind me but didn't let it latch, in case I had to bust out of there fast. The small apartment was just as it had been the day before. The only difference was that Tonio wasn't playing Halo 2.

The controller was neatly tucked away on a shelf beneath the TV. I'd never seen a boy do that. When my brothers weren't playing they would just leave the thing attached to the set, the better to trip over the wires every chance you got. A worn beige blanket was folded and set squarely on a pillow at one end of the sofa. Was this where Tonio slept?

Sylvia and Tonio were very tidy, that was for sure. I glanced again at the humane society calendar tacked to the wall, noted again the words "Tonio—Shooting" written carefully in every box until the end of the month. For that day it said shooting was at 6:00 A.M. Could Tonio still be at shooting practice, or whatever it was?

Something else was different: The black pug wasn't there. Maybe Tonio had taken him with him.

With three steps I was in the kitchen. I passed the small wooden table where Chelsea had set the ring with the missing center stone, but it was gone. The yellow daisies, still in their jelly jar, were beginning to wilt; no one had added water since I'd been there. The pile of unopened mail I'd spied the day before was untouched.

Just as I was about to turn to go, a man's voice said, "Is there something I can help you with?"

I jumped so high I can't believe I didn't hit my head on the ceiling. Until that moment I hadn't realized how truly scared I'd been snooping around this strange girl's apartment. I spun around. "Who are you?" I sputtered. The words just popped out. The man was wearing a uniform—light blue shirt, dark pants, dark tie, thick utility belt with one of those big black sticks—but he wasn't a cop, he was a security guard. On one arm there was a big patch that said AMES SECURITY. Over his pocket was an oval name patch that said SHARK.

"You work for Ames?" I said. "My brother used to work there." This was a complete lie, but I had to say something, to show he hadn't practically given me a heart attack.

Shark chuckled. "Sorry, didn't mean to startle you."

I pegged him at about the same age as my brother, which meant old but not so old that you couldn't imagine being that age one day. He was tall and thin, with terrible posture. He had long pale eyes and a mustache. He smiled at me, but I could tell it was a mask beneath which he was sizing me up.

He'd come from the bedroom. He had a cheap flowered cosmetics bag in his hand, turned halfway inside out.

"Is Tonio around?" I asked.

He chuckled some more. What was so funny? His sleeves were rolled up to his elbow. His forearms were as big as that cartoon sailor named Popeye. "You one of Tonio's lady friends?"

"Kind of," I said.

"He's not here. Name's Shark by the way." He stuck out his hand for me to shake.

"I figured." I nodded toward his name patch.

I shook his hand, but it was as if I was with Reggie, and he'd dared me to touch some dead thing he'd found in the backyard. Suddenly, I missed Reggie. Why wasn't he here having this strange encounter with me? Oh, I know, because it was more important for him to hang out with that twit Amanda the Panda. I felt myself starting to lose my grip on the situation.

"And what's your name?" he asked.

"Suzanne," I said. Suzanne is my middle name, so I wasn't totally lying.

"How long have you been seeing Tonio? I didn't think he had a girlfriend. Or not a serious one, anyway." Again, the fake smile. Didn't he just ask whether I was one of Tonio's girlfriends, plural, which means one of many? I seriously did not like the way this was going. Why hadn't I left the door wide open behind me? Outside, I could hear the sound of skateboard wheels coasting down the plywood ramp. Suddenly, it seemed like the most fun in the world.

"I don't know. A while. Where's Sylvia? Maybe she knows where he is."

"She must be out," he said.

The question was, of course, what in the heck was he doing here? "Are you the house sitter? Tonio said they might be going out of town on vacation."

This time Shark really laughed. Just as I was about to

write him off as a harmless dork he said, "You got it, Suzanne, Sylvia's gone away on a Hawaiian cruise and I'm the house sitter." He grinned at me again, pleased with his sarcasm. I was always a little unnerved when any grown-up besides my brothers was sarcastic with me.

There was nothing else for me to do but be on my way. I moved toward the door, and half expected him to block my escape. He stepped aside, and as he did, I could see through the tiny hallway into the bedroom. It was obviously Sylvia's room, with a comforter splashed with big pink and orange flowers.

All her dresser drawers were hanging open. I tried not to look shocked, or like I cared much. It was obvious that I'd interrupted him in the process of turning the apartment upside down. The rest of the apartment was so neat because he'd just started when I'd walked in.

Shark saw me notice this and took two big steps and pulled open the door. He wanted me out of there.

"I'll tell Tonio you stopped by, Suzanne. I'm sure he'll be sad he missed you."

- 7 -

I was so glad to be home I offered to make Minerva's Special Deviled Eggs. Mark Clark had broken out the barbecue, in celebration of the arrival of summer. He was going to grill some ribs and chicken and corn on the cob. Morgan was in the kitchen chopping carrots for Morgan's Special Chopped Salad. Have you noticed how everything we cook has a name, and usually includes the word "special"? In truth, it's just regular food, but we like it.

I put on a dozen eggs to boil in a big pot, then fetched myself a cold Mountain Dew from the fridge. I put ice in a glass anyway. Sometimes, when I have to think, I like chewing on ice. It's supposed to be bad for your teeth, but I don't care.

It was warm in the kitchen. The late-afternoon sun

beat through the row of dining room windows and through the door leading into the kitchen. We live on a slight hill, so we don't have any curtains there. I'd let Jupiter out of his cage so he could stretch his legs. "Stretch his legs" was Clark code for allowing Jupiter to crawl inside the small hole beneath the cupboard and romp around. We could hear the thumps and bumps of him galloping in the dark among the pans and plates.

"I see you survived your electronics class," said Mark Clark. He was standing in front of the sink shucking corn, dropping the pale green husks into a brown paper garbage bag beside him.

"It was actually pretty cool. I mean, boring in a lot of ways, and the teacher, Mr. Lawndale, is a complete loon, but we got to blow up these things called capacitors."

"Yeah, baby," said Morgan, doing his Austin Powers impersonation. "Could this by chance be because your prof didn't have your undivided attention?"

"I guess," I said.

"It's an old trick to get kids to take electricity seriously."

"I take electricity seriously!" I said.

There was a moment of silence in which I imagined that my brothers and I all contemplated the electric shock that had basically made me more confident, but also more stubborn.

To break the silence I told about the breadboards and sticking the wire legs of capacitors, which looked like alien bugs, into the positive and negative holes, and not knowing—because we weren't listening—that if you stick the long leg into the negative you'll wind up with an explosion.

"The little ones are fun, but if you get a huge capacitor—like say from a computer power supply or something—you could blow the roof off." Mark Clark chuckled. I added "the love of blowing stuff up" to skateboarding on my mental list of things boys never outgrow.

The eggs finished boiling and I plucked out the yolks and mashed them in a bowl with a fork. Morgan and Mark Clark started trading stories, first about various capacitor explosions and then about other cool things they've blown up over the years. They forgot all about me, which was fine, because it gave me a chance to think.

As far as I could tell, Sylvia had returned to her apartment with Chelsea's ring, but then hadn't been home since. My main clue was the mail sitting on the table, still unopened. Everyone opened their mail when they got home, didn't they? Maybe she bought the ring, came home and pried the red diamond from the center, got in her car, and took off. If she had a car. It wasn't like you could take MAX to the Mexican border.

The only problem with this theory was, was she the type of person to leave her little brother behind? The folded blanket and pillow set on the corner of the couch meant that either he was living there or staying there. I'd heard of fathers leaving the family, and mothers leaving like mine did, but never brothers and sisters. Usually, if you were left in the care of your older brother or sister, they took their responsibilities seriously.

Maybe I was totally jumping to conclusions. Maybe Sylvia had spent the night at a friend's house, or had gone out of town somewhere for the weekend. The thing about trying to solve a mystery was that while you had to see what was right in front of your face, you had to be careful not to read more into it than was there. For example, running into Shark the security guard, who acted as if he had every right to be in the apartment. It seemed as if he'd been going through Sylvia's stuff, but maybe not. Maybe, she just had a really messy bedroom and made Tonio keep the rest of the place clean.

I sprinkled paprika on top of my deviled eggs, wondering as I always do whether paprika has any taste, or if it's just for decoration. No one seems to know. Quills helped me set the picnic table, even though technically setting the table was my job. Morgan asked me what kind of salad dressing I wanted on my chopped salad. Mark Clark was pouring the drinks, and asked, as he always did, whether I wanted milk or juice. I reminded

him it was the weekend, when I got to have soda with
my meals.

It was 7:30 or 8:00. The sun had dropped behind the
other side of the house, leaving us in a chilly shadow. We
had just started passing the food around when I remembered Jupiter, still racing around behind the kitchen
cupboards, his own private obstacle course. I excused
myself and went into the house to find him. He was inside the cabinet where we keep the plates and bowls, sitting on the top dinner dish washing his paws.

I dropped Jupiter back in his cage behind the piano
in the living room. Suddenly, the phone rang in the
kitchen. My brothers and I all have cell phones. No one
ever calls on the landline except our dad, who spends
most of his time doing his lawyer work out of town,
mostly in Los Angeles. Dad calls often when he's travel-
ing, so I figured it was him. I answered the phone.

"Hi, Charlie." Dad's real name was Howard, but we
called him Charlie after the boss you never saw in *Charlie's Angels*. It was a dumb family joke that cracked us up
anyway.

"Charlie! Is this the Clark residence?" I was surprised
to hear my mom's voice. I'd forgotten that Mark Clark
said Mom was coming home next week. It was sort of
sad that I'd forgotten, but Mom had been planning on
coming home about a dozen times over the past year and
she never had.

"Um, yes it is." Why didn't I just say "Hi, Mom, it's me!" Why did I pretend I didn't recognize her voice?

"Minerva? Is that you, honey?"

"Oh, hi, Mom."

"Hi, honey! I can't wait to see you. I'll be home Sunday."

"Me too you, Mom."

"I've got big plans for us—and a surprise, too."

"Are you bringing me a pony?" This was an old joke from when I was small. Every time she and my dad went somewhere together, and would call home and say they had something for me, I wondered if it was a pony. It was an inside joke with my mom, I thought, but she just kept right on chattering.

"You don't know the *meaning* of quality time, Minnow. We're going to have so much fun together."

"Cool," I said. That familiar feeling as if a ghost were ironing my insides flat crept up on me. I did not think it was cool. I wished I was on my cell, then I could say she was breaking up.

"I was thinking we all could go to the coast for a few days. Do you have a boyfriend or anything?"

"Uh . . ." I said. "What do you mean?" A boyfriend! No, I did not have a boyfriend. I had an almost-boyfriend who had not called me. The fact Kevin had not called me made me crush on him even more. What was with that? I'd checked my phone about twenty-seven hundred times that day. I fished my phone out of my back pocket and checked it again. No messages. My mom didn't notice I hadn't answered.

"I remember when I was your age, my parents always wanted to take us camping and I never wanted to leave my boyfriend."

"Well, I am taking a class."

"But you'll be able to miss it, won't you?"

"I don't think they like you to miss."

"Well, I'm sure they'd understand. So what else is going on there?"

"We're sort of in the middle of dinner."

"You're making healthy food choices I hope."

"Got a plate of steamed broccoli sitting out there getting cold as we speak."

"Great! That's one of my favorite snacks. Although I don't think I could eat a whole plate of it. I always said you were just like me."

I hoped not.

We chatted for a few more years about making a pilgrimage to Claire's, and resisting the temptation to stop at Cinnabon. From the sound of it, she had every minute of every day planned. She wanted us to get up early and go to a mother/daughter yoga class taught by a friend of hers in the Pearl District. We talked for a few more minutes about eighth grade, and she wondered whether it was too early to go school clothes shopping. I reminded her we wore uniforms at Holy Family. Before we hung up she said, "Don't forget, I've got a big big surprise!"

I know every kid my age thinks their parents are strange, but my mom really *is* strange. She's like someone who's had a spell cast on her and thinks that this very moment in time is the only moment that exists, that there was never a past, when she and my dad were married and had four children. Morgan once said that's because our mom is trying to live in the Now. Quills snorted and said it was because she felt guilty about leaving us, but couldn't admit it, because then she would have to admit she was wrong. I secretly believe Quills is right, but I didn't like anyone to say anything bad about her.

The weird part of her Living in the Now business, though, is that she never likes anybody to change. She thinks of us all as we were in the Way Back When. She has my brothers and me fixed at certain ages, and that's how we always are. Mark Clark liked to play "office" when he was in first grade, and to her, being a computer genius is just a grown-up version of playing office. Quills used to sing into the end of a hairbrush in front of the mirror, so it was no surprise that he wanted to be a world-famous rock singer. When Morgan was little, he used to pick up rocks and stare at all the tiny creatures that lived beneath it. Somehow she connects that with being a Buddhist, but I can't remember how. Anyway, I am her sensitive, tender blossom (don't laugh!) because I used to cry when the buttons would fall off my jackets. I really didn't think she'd like the post-electric shock-mystery solving me, who hardly ever cried at all anymore.

It was easier not to think about my mom at all, and most of the time, I didn't.

After dinner, I did the dishes, including drying the pans too big for the dishwasher.

I did not check my phone messages.

I did not calculate how many hours until Kevin, who I was starting to realize had totally lead me on, was coming back from Fly-Fishingville, Montana.

I got a Dove Bar out of the freezer, even though I was stuffed. One advantage of thinking you're great the way you are is that one more little zit doesn't make any difference.

I decided I hated Kevin, and wouldn't think about him anymore, ever again.

I marched up to my room and checked my e-mail, to see if maybe Kevin had e-mailed me.

Nothing. Now I truly despised him.

I ate my ice cream and IMed Reggie. At least Reggie never lead me on and said I had cool wild hair like the surfer chick girls in Maui.

Ferretluver: So how would you get rid of a diamond?

BorntobeBored: Give it to an evil girlfriend and wait until she breaks up with you?
Ferretluver: LOL.

I waited a few minutes. Reggie had the most active on-line life of anyone I knew. He was probably IMing two or three other people. Or just Amanda the Panda. I tugged my rebus notebook out of my top drawer, flipped through the pages.

CI II (see eye to eye) and ROOD (back door) were among my most recent ones, and they struck me as really easy and babyish. I wanted to make some full sentence rebuses that included drawings, but I couldn't draw. Kevin could draw, of course, but I was never speaking to him again.

BorntobeBored: Who's got a diamond they want to get rid of?
Ferretluver: It was that red one I was telling you about. If you were trying to sell it, where would you go?
BorntobeBored: You couldn't sell it.
Ferretluver: ????
BorntobeBored: They're just too dang rare. It would draw too much attention to itself. You'd need a fence.
Ferretluver: Whaz that?

BorntobeBored: Miss Law & Order Addict doesn't know what a fence is?

Ferretluver: *embarrassed*

BorntobeBored: A fence is the guy who receives the stolen stuff, then sells it to the right people who won't attract attention.

Ferretluver: *light bulb goes on* So what are you doing right now?

I waited for an answer, but never got one. I glanced back down at my rebus notebook.

When I read the rebus that said NHAPPY (unhappy without you), I closed the notebook.

I glanced at my screen and saw I had a new IM. Someone named **Bryceyoyo**. Bryce Duncan?

Bryceyoyo: thought mebbe you'd be out blowing stuff up!

Ferretluver: Where'd u get my address?

Bryceyoyo: the class list. teacher dude passed around that sheet, remember?

Ferretluver: Duh. I was too busy snoooozing.

Bryceyoyo: whatcha up to?

Ferretluver: Trying to figure out who might have stolen a red diamond.

Bryceyoyo: hey, wait a minute, aren't you that girl

who helped the cops catch a murderer or some-
thing?
Ferretluver: Yup yup
Bryceyoyo: *whistles* awesum!

And then I did the exact thing I hollered at Chelsea for
doing. I told Bryce Duncan all about finding Sylvia
Soto by searching through the garbage at Coffee People, and how we tracked her down, and saw that the
diamond had been taken from the center of the ring,
and how now Sylvia was probably missing. I told him
about Tonio, and how suspicious he'd acted when
Chelsea and I had asked about his sister, and about
returning to the apartment only to run into the house
sitter Shark, who was so clearly *not* the house sitter,
who was a security guard, who may or may not have
been turning the place upside down, looking for . . .
what? A stolen diamond?

Bryce Duncan (like Mark Clark, Bryce Duncan was
one of those people who for some reason begged to be
called by two names) said he heard that security guards
are always applying to be cops, but the cops don't want
them because they're too eager to draw their weapons
and shoot up the place. I LOLed, but felt creeped out at
the same time.

I heard muffled noises in the rest of the house, the
brothers settling in to watch a movie downstairs in the

TV room, then after some time, the pipes knocking the way they do when the shower goes on.

Bryce Duncan asked questions. He was almost as funny as Reggie, but not quite. He wondered who the red diamond was for. That was a good question I hadn't thought of. Who *was* the diamond for? Louis de Guzman made jewelry for a lot of rich people in Portland. Was this for a ring for the mayor's wife, or someone like that?

Finally, it seemed very late.

Bryceyoyo: so i was wonderin, you have the e-mail or number for Jenna?
Ferretluver: ????
Bryceyoyo: that uberhottie in our class.
Ferretluver: What about the stupid class list? Isn't that how you got my e-mail??????
Bryceyoyo: can't read the girl's handwriting.

For some reason, it was reassuring that Bryce Duncan was crushing on the girl in the newsboy hat from basic electronics. She was cute in the standard cute girl mode. It made perfect sense why he would want her number. There was no mystery of love and attraction at all.

I logged off, brushed my teeth, and went to bed. Why had I told all that stuff to stupid Bryce Duncan? I tossed and turned. I fell asleep trying to tell myself that it wasn't as bad as blabbing to the owner of a pawn shop. It wasn't as if Bryce the Yo-Yo was suddenly going to launch into his own search for the rare red diamond. Still, I felt awful. I kicked off my comforter, tugged the sheet up around my chin. It was stuffy in my room.

Suddenly, I sat up in the dark.

Bryce asked who the diamond was for. Who *was* the diamond for? Whoever it was, he or she would have known Mr. de Guzman was bringing it into the country. He would have known the day it was set to arrive, and he may have also known that Mr. de Guzman wasn't transporting the gem the normal way, but hiding it in plain sight in his daughter's cheap glass ring. And if he knew all that . . . then what? Then maybe he told someone else, who was either Sylvia Soto, or knew Sylvia Soto, and she thought she'd nab the diamond for herself. One thing was for sure: There was at least one other person who knew when the red diamond was arriving in Portland, and I had to find him.

The next morning, after I did my chores, I borrowed Morgan's mountain bike and rode to the de Guzmans'. They lived about a mile from us, thirty blocks, give or take, and it was all downhill, through a string of neighborhoods with wide shady streets. Mark Clark, who loved telling me stories about how much he rode his bike when he was growing up, was thrilled to pieces.

I made a point of avoiding the street where I'd seen the hawk speeding away with the baby opossum in its talons. I've heard birds have neighborhoods just like everyone else.

The sprinklers were on at the de Guzmans'. They had a perfect, cushiony jewel-green front lawn. There were no cars in the driveway. It looked as if no one was home.

Still, I leaned my bike against the side of the house and went to the front door. Even though I could have called on my cell, sometimes it's better just to show up and see what happens. That was something else I learned from watching detective shows. The detectives almost never call first.

Seconds after I rang the bell, from deep in the house, I could hear the scrabble of what sounded like a hundred doggie toenails on the wood floor. I smiled just thinking of Winkin', Blinkin', and especially Ned, who didn't quite fit in. Through the door I recognized the voice of Mrs. de Guzman. She was hollering, "Boys boys boys! Stop it right now!" There were two long panes of glass on either side of the door, and through them I could see the dogs jumping all over each other, and Mrs. de Guzman with her red hair and gold jewelry trying to shush them with no success at all.

She opened the door just wide enough to peek out, but the dogs escaped anyway. They ran around like wind-up toys, scampered around the wet lawn barking madly at the sprinkler. As soon as the stream of water rotated back in our direction, the dogs started biting the water. I burst out laughing, and so did Mrs. de Guzman, even though, at the same time, she was shrieking: "Blinkin', *no*!" or "Neddie, no no *no*. Stop that!"

"Hey, Ned! Here, Ned!" I could not help myself. I bent down and slapped my thighs and he came bounding over and—ha ha!—jumped straight into my arms. He licked my face. He smelled like fancy shampoo and wet dog.

"Ned," shrieked Mrs. de Guzman, "you know better than that!"

"Nah," I said, "my fault."

"That dog is a loverboy, that's for sure," said Mrs. de Guzman, shaking her head.

I helped her round up Winkin' and Blinkin', whom I could not even tell apart, and by the time they were all back in the house, I was soaked.

"Good Lord! Come inside and let's get you toweled off. I'm *so* sorry . . ."

Like most moms I know, she was speedy and efficient. She was everywhere at once, racing through the house and chatting at the same time, her gold bracelets dangling on her bony wrist. Mrs. de Guzman's copper penny red hair was needle straight. It swung around her small head as she threw open the French doors that lead to the backyard, Winkin', Blinkin', and Ned bustling around her ankles, then raced back out of the kitchen to another part of the house, talking all the while.

"Normally these dogs are more well-behaved. They're show dogs, but even show dogs need to be exercised regularly. Our dog person is a terrific guy, but he's not the most reliable young man on earth. He's one of those poor souls who needs a few jobs just to get by, and sometimes he shows up late, or not at all. Louis thinks we should get rid of him. And Ned. You don't want a dog, do you?"

"Well, yeah," I blurted out.

She smiled. "Let me get you that towel."

While she was out of the room I took the opportunity to snoop around a little. In our kitchen we had a desk shoved in the back corner where the adults sat and wrote out bills. It was also a holder for old mail and catalogs. I was hoping I'd catch a glimpse of a bill or a letter or a note, something that would give me a clue who the red diamond had been meant for. I glanced around. There was nothing out of place, no stacks of papers, no pencil holders, nothing ugly.

Mrs. de Guzman hurried back into the room with a fluffy white towel and handed it to me.

"Can I pour you some coffee, hon? Or, do you drink coffee yet? I don't think it's good for you girls, but Chelsea loves her lattes, and when I was a girl in the South we drank coffee with chicory—"

"That sounds good," I said. I didn't know what chicory was. Maybe it was like cinnamon?

"Oh Minerva, it was! We loved our chicory."

She pulled out two blue coffee mugs and set them on the counter. Mrs. de Guzman was obviously one of those grown-ups who enjoyed hearing herself talk, which was fine by me.

"Do you know when Chelsea will be home?"

"Not for a while, I'm afraid. She and her dad are playing eighteen holes this morning. Cream and sugar? It's a terrible habit to get into, cream and sugar, nothing but empty calories. But it's the only way to drink coffee at your age, right?"

"You read my mind."

Mrs. de Guzman laughed, too. When she smiled, I saw she had some lipstick smeared on her front tooth. "Well, at least I can read someone's mind! Between my daughter and my husband . . . well, it's been a little tense around here since we returned from London. Chelsea told you about our little situation?"

"Yeah, she did," I said.

Mrs. de Guzman disappeared into the pantry for a moment and returned with some of those crumbly wedge-shaped cookies called biscotti. I hid a smile. Quills called biscotti Human Dog Biscuits.

"Louis is fit to be tied, of course, but it's his own fault. He's been doing this for decades, trying to avoid

paying the exorbitant prices Brinks charges for transport, and insurance, customs clearance. Of course, he
also does it for the sheer fun of it. I've carried diamonds
into the country in my dental floss case before! Anyway,
this is the chance he took not using the proper chan-
nels." She took a sip of her coffee and sighed. "I do
miss my chicory."

"I've heard those red diamonds are really rare and
valuable."

"Ohhhhh, yes," she said.

"The person whose ring it was for must be, like,
really upset," I said. It was a lame thing to say, but I
didn't want the conversation to veer back into Mrs. de
Guzman's girlhood coffee-drinking experiences. I took
a small sip of coffee. Ugh.

Mrs. de Guzman rolled her eyes. "Well, that's the
silly thing. It's not as if the diamond was for a girl's
engagement ring, or even an anniversary or eternity
ring. It was for Rodney von Lager's new movie."

Rodney von Lager was a local Portland guy who
made independent films. Mostly, they were shot here in
town using real people as actors. He was famous for being anti-Hollywood, but every once in a while he would
make a big Hollywood movie that would get nominated
for an Academy Award, which made him more famous.
But he always came back to Portland.

"I heard he was shooting something here this summer.

My brother's band played a few songs for that movie he did, *53 Miles West of Venus*. Quills thought it would mean a record deal for his band, but the movie pretty much sank like a stone."

"Chelsea didn't mention your brother had a band. Would I know it?"

"Humongous Bag of Cashews?"

"Of course." I could tell she'd never heard of it, but she was somebody's mom, and part of her job was to be polite and encouraging.

"The diamond was for his movie?" I didn't understand. Why would a movie director famous for making artsy low-budget movies need a real diamond?

"He's doing an urban remake of *Lord of the Rings* with street kids. Is that right? Louis knows better than I do. He needed a red diamond for the ring."

"A real red diamond? Isn't that kind of . . ." I didn't know what the word was. Out of character? Ridiculous?

Mrs. de Guzman must have read my mind again. "It's pure madness. But apparently Rodney von Lager is known for 'keeping it real.'" She made quotes with her fingers. "He wanted a real red diamond in the ring mostly to inspire the greed and wonder in his actors. In one of his other movies he shot in a house that was supposed to be like the one he grew up in. There was a window in one of the coat closets, and he delayed the start of production to have an identical window installed in that closet. And here's evidence of the von Lager madness—*in the movie, they never open the closet door.*"

"So you mean no one ever sees the window?"

"No, ma'am. An absolute waste of money, in my book. I grew up in Louisiana without a pot to piss in— excuse me, but you get my point—and this just burns me up."

I poured some more milk into my coffee, took another polite sip. Sure, it was bizarre, but I'd heard stories like this before about perfectionist film directors. The bigger question for me was, how did he know Sylvia Soto? Was she working on the movie? Was she his neighbor? His nanny? His girlfriend? Somehow Sylvia knew to be at the airport the day the de Guzmans arrived. Somehow she knew to shadow Chelsea, and to offer to buy her ring straight off her finger. But how?

"Is Rodney von Lager filming in Portland?" I asked.

"Under the Burnside Bridge. The skate park there, I believe. That's the last I heard, anyway. I'm not sure if this situation with the lost diamond has halted production, or what. I overheard Louis suggest that he could rent von Lager a ring from the store—of course, it wouldn't have a red diamond in it, the best Louis could do would be blue or champagne—but von Lager wasn't interested. Those artistic types are so particular. More coffee, honey?"

She talked more about the dogs and their special diets,

and how much work they were, but Louis loved them, well, except Ned, who had a lovely nature, but had disappointed in other ways. I smiled and asked a question here and there. I think Mrs. de Guzman was lonely. She asked me where I was going to go to high school. She asked if I thought Chelsea was too thin. I tried to listen and be polite, but beneath the kitchen counter, where Mrs. de Guzman couldn't see, my legs were bouncing like mad.

Even though Chelsea was off playing golf with her dad, I decided to check out the set. I could be there in ten minutes.

Finally my T-shirt was dry and I'd eaten my Human Dog Biscuit and we'd run out of things to talk about. Outside, through the French doors, I could see Winkin', Blinkin', and Ned, lying on their sides, snoring in the sun. Mrs. de Guzman walked me to the door and told me not to be a stranger. She stood in the doorway of her huge white house waving as I sped off down the street.

Burnside is a long street at the heart of the city that begins in a hilly wooded area west of downtown, runs down a steep hill into a fancy shopping district, then on into Old Town, past the Salvation Army and a bunch of old brick warehouses. On top of the last warehouse before you reach the Willamette River sits the huge neon MADE IN OREGON sign, Portland's famous landmark.

Every night the white outline of our state, with a leaping elk in the center, shines over our city. Burnside becomes a bridge as it passes over the river. A world-famous skate park was tucked beneath the east side of the bridge, not far from Chelsea's house. I knew right where it was.

At a stoplight I called Mark Clark and told him Chelsea and I were going to the mall. I didn't like the mall, but I was glad they invented it. Adults believed girls my age could spend every waking minute there, so it was always a handy excuse.

The light turned green. I pedaled a few more blocks down Martin Luther King Jr. Boulevard, before turning right down a narrow cobblestoned street. Down the hill, I could see the movie set two blocks away. A row of those huge silver movie-set buses were parked at the curb across from the skate park.

The skate park was a swimming pool–like structure whose concrete sides rose up to enclose a collection of vertical ramps, runs, bowls, and keyholes. The curvy stretches of concrete were painted lime green, splattered with random drips of red, pink, and turquoise. This was the best place to skate in all of the northwest; shady and cool in the summer, sheltered from the rain in the winter.

There were clusters of people here and there. Lights rose up on skinny poles above their heads. Once, Quills took me on the set of *53 Miles West of Venus* and one thing that struck me was how everyone looked alike. The camera people and the sound people and the assistant-type people all wore grubby jeans, T-shirts, grody old Jack Purcell tennis shoes or cowboy boots. The actors looked exactly the same way. No one acting in the movie was dressed as a pirate, or a private eye, or in an evening gown. The only way you could tell the difference between the people making the movie and the people *in* the movie, was that the people making the movie had walkie-talkies on their belts.

It was the same situation with this movie, *The Dude of the Rings.* Everyone here looked like they came from the same nation of semi-grungy art majors.

My plan had been to simply watch, and to formulate a plan while I was watching. While I was riding my bike from the de Guzmans' house I started thinking that Rodney von Lager had maybe hired Sylvia to buy the ring off Chelsea. Or maybe Sylvia and Rodney were partners. Rodney von Lager liked to be thought of as edgy. I remember Quills telling me that in *53 Miles West of Venus* one of the actors was someone who'd just gotten out of prison for robbing a bank. He wasn't a very good actor, but Rodney thought it gave him street cred. Given this, it made perfect sense to me that Rodney von Lager would snitch the red diamond, rather than pay Mr. de Guzman for it.

The problem was, no one in this big crowd of people looked anything like how Chelsea described Sylvia Soto.

I recognized Rodney von Lager from the time Quills took me to visit the set of *Venus*. He had the greasiest hair of all, graying and shoulder length, but was still sort of handsome in that male-model-who-could-use-a-shower sort of way.

He stood in the middle of three boys, explaining something with his hands. They stood in the parking lot next to the park. I couldn't see who he was talking to, but one of the people had a black pug with a rope tied around his neck. The black pug wandered around, getting his rope wrapped around people's legs. Rodney stepped aside to disentangle himself, and I couldn't believe my eyes.

It was Tonio, Sylvia's brother, and the dog with the rope around his neck was Tonio's black pug.

I don't think my mouth dropped open as I stared and stared. Maybe it did. I'd stopped in the middle of the sidewalk, next to the lot where Rodney von Lager was directing his actors, my feet on either side of the bike, gripping the handlebars. What was Tonio doing here? I scanned the crowd again for Sylvia, but there was no Sylvia. Suddenly, I flashed on the calendar on the wall of their apartment, and all the days that said "Tonio—Shooting." It wasn't shooting practice for a summer basketball league. Tonio had a role in *The Dude of the*

Rings. Maybe it wasn't Rodney and Sylvia who were partners, but Tonio and Sylvia. Sylvia didn't need to be on the set, or know Rodney personally. Here was her brother, on Rodney's set every single day. Suddenly, my stomach hurt.

A small angry girl was marching toward me. She wore her dyed black hair in tiny, angry pigtails. She'd been yelling something at me.

"You'll have to move, we're getting ready to shoot. Excuse me! Miss! We're shooting a movie here. You'll have to move."

Before I could say anything, Rodney, and then Tonio, looked my way to see what the commotion was.

Tonio raised his dark eyebrows in what could only be recognition.

- 8 -

I **must have** stood there looking as if I'd just arrived from another solar system. The small angry girl with the tiny black pigtails motioned me across the street. "You can watch from over there." Then she sighed, shook her head dramatically, so I couldn't miss the point that I was the biggest idiot she'd come across in a long time.

I walked my bike across the street, to where another small knot of people were standing on the sidewalk, opposite the skate park. They were not movie people, but probably friends of the actors, or else people who'd stopped to watch. A lady—she could only be someone's mom, in her pink polo, blue cotton skirt, and enormous sunglasses—was snapping pictures with her digital camera.

We watched Rodney direct the three boys, including

Tonio. He was gesturing with his big hands, then stopped suddenly and held up a finger. He pulled his cell phone from where it was clipped on the belt loop of his jeans and chatted away. The boys stood there, waiting. Tonio picked up the black pug and rubbed the top of his head with his knuckles, staring intently at Rodney von Lager as he talked on the phone.

I watched Tonio watch Rodney talk on the phone. That was how it was with cell phones: People said anything, right out in public, no matter who was listening. What if Mr. de Guzman called Rodney and they talked about the diamond—when and how it was arriving— and Tonio just stood there quietly soaking up the information? Then he went home and told his sister.

Rodney flipped his phone shut, gave a few more instructions, then joined the cameraman behind the camera.

He didn't yell "Action!" but somehow the boys knew to stride into the skate park. They all carried skateboards and wore black knee pads over their jeans, held on with silver duct tape. Then one of the boys—smaller than either Tonio or the other boy and wearing a bright white T-shirt—stopped before the gate, and they argued. Then he walked away. Then Rodney yelled cut. Then they did it again, and again.

"Why are they doing so many takes?" asked someone.

"Rodney is a perfectionist," said the mom with the

digital camera. "He may not look like one, but he is. He's a true artist." She sighed.

Our group then began discussing how the scene they were shooting related to *The Lord of the Rings*. One sweaty, red-faced runner in T-shirt and shorts, who'd stop to watch, said he thought the three boys were members of the good street gang. They were like the three hobbits, aligned with the elves, the dwarves, and the other forces for good in *The Lord of the Rings*. They just wanted everyone to live in harmony and skate and have fun. There was also a bad street gang who wanted to run the good street gang out of the skate park. They were like the goblins, orcs, and other forces of darkness. I think Tonio was supposed to be like the hobbit Sam Gamgee, the one who was always following Frodo around like a nervous babysitter. I wasn't sure who, exactly, the black pug was supposed to be. Golem maybe?

I wasn't listening and didn't care. Mrs. de Guzman's coffee was churning in my stomach. I imagined it looked like some prehistoric tar pit in there. About half a block away they were setting up lunch beneath a big white tent, and the smell of grilled meat drifted our way and made me feel sicker yet. The film crew was shooting in the shade, but we spectators were stuck on the white sidewalk, baking. I tried to focus, tried to think: What does this all mean?

I wasn't very good at thinking on my feet. I was like Jupiter, who, once he found a treasure—one of my old My Little Ponies, or a chewing gum wrapper—hid it in a secret spot, to be examined later.

A few things made no sense. First, if Tonio and Sylvia were partners in crime, why hadn't Sylvia been home since yesterday? That left me with the she's-taken-off-with-the-gem theory, but I still didn't think a big sister would do that to a little brother, especially since it looked as if Sylvia was in charge of Tonio, the same way my brothers were in charge of me. Second, what about Shark, the security guard guy? What was he doing in Sylvia's apartment when she wasn't there? Not house-sitting, that's for sure.

I wondered if maybe Shark was working security on the movie, but knew somehow in my bones that that would be too neat. Still, I scanned the crowd for any uniforms. Aside from two Portland police officers leaning against their car, I didn't see any other security-type people.

I had a stomachache. I had a headache. I was hot. I needed to get home, now, so I could sort things out.

Just as I cranked the front wheel of my bike around to leave, I heard Rodney call for a lunch break. Tonio bounded across the street, making a beeline in my direction. He wore baggy jeans with torn knees and a green army jacket. I started to pedal off.

"Hey," said Tonio. I kept going, hoping he would think that I hadn't heard him. "Dude, you still lookin' for my sis?"

I stopped. "Your sister Sylvia?"

"Only have the one."

I laughed, even though it wasn't really funny. My heart was beating hard. "Oh, right. I guess she's home now?"

"Don't know. She hasn't been home in like a couple of days. I thought maybe you'd seen her. Normally she calls. I thought you and that other girl might have caught up with her or something."

"No, not yet," I said.

"Hey, I gotta eat. You want to . . ." He started walking toward the white tent, where two long tables of food were set end to end. I followed along behind.

"It's cool you're in a movie," I said.

He shrugged, took a plate from a stack at the end of the table, and started inching down the food line, helping himself to grilled sausages, roasted potatoes, and salad. I trailed along at his shoulder. "How did you get the role?"

"Rodney came to school. He likes working with real kids, I guess."

"When was the last time Sylvia was home?"

"It's so not like her. She normally calls me like every hour, man." He glanced over at me then. I felt as if he was really looking at me for the first time. "I thought you and that other girl were like her friends."

"No, we don't know her." I took a breath to steady myself. "My friend sold her a ring by mistake. We were hoping to get it back."

Tonio stuck a piece of bread on the side of his plate and grabbed a handful of silver-wrapped butter squares sitting in a small bowl. I looked at his profile, his long black eyelashes and perfect triangular-shaped nose.

"I don't know anything about that," he said. I couldn't tell whether he was telling the truth or not. He wasn't easy to read. I could not get over how much older Tonio seemed than the other boys I knew. There was something *sorrowful* about him, like the worst day of his life hadn't washed over him like it did with most kids, but had dragged him out to sea, where he floated, lost.

"Do you know what ring I mean?" I persisted. We moved down the line, me at his shoulder. The girl behind him in line gave me a strange look.

"Nah, Sylvia loves jewelry. She's got a million rings and bracelets. I just don't get it. Even when she spends the night over with that boyfriend of hers, she tells me, you know? So I don't go worrying. She calls me. No matter what." He shook his head slowly, rearranged the silver butter pats so they wouldn't fall off the edge of his plate.

"Sylvia has a boyfriend?" A lame question that wasn't really a question, but it would keep him talking.

"She met him at the humane society, where we got

Chichi." He nodded over to where the black pug was sitting on someone's lap. "The guy's okay, but I can tell he's trying to get on my good side. Nice, but phony nice, like he wants something. He told me once as a joke that he volunteers at the humane society just to pick up chicks. 'Girls really dig a guy who loves animals,' he says. He dates my sister and he's telling me this?" We were at the end of the buffet. He leaned down and grabbed a cold can of Dr Pepper from an ice chest.

Suddenly, I thought of too-nice Shark, holding what had to be Sylvia's cosmetic case, turned half inside out, smiling in a way that looking back seemed phony nice indeed.

"Is her boyfriend a security guard?"

Tonio raised his dark eyebrows. "Yeah, how'd you know?' "

I was saved from having to say how I knew by the short boy in the white T-shirt playing the Frodo character who strode over on his short bowed legs. He looked older up close—maybe in his twenties—and couldn't have been more than five feet tall. Like Tonio's, his plate was piled high with as much food as he could fit on it. Hanging on a thick silver chain around his neck was a ring. The ring of the title, I guessed, set with a huge red stone in its center. It was as big as a marble. It looked like a piece of cinnamon candy.

"Nice ring," I said. "That's, uh, not real is it?"

KAREN KARBO

"You like it?" he said. Frodo had a deep voice and some type of East Coast accent, and a big smile that made his whole face crinkle up. His blond hair curled over his ears.

"Sure," I said. "It's . . . big."

He took it off the chain around his neck and tossed it at me. "It's yours. Compliments of another fine Rodney von Lager production."

"Wow. Thanks," I said. I was completely confused. "Don't you need it?"

Tonio laughed. "We got about a hundred of those."

"It's a piece of junk," said Frodo.

"That's bizarre," I said. "I thought Rodney von Lager was all about being authentic and stuff. This is so . . ."

"Big and fake?" said Frodo.

"Well, yeah. You'd think he'd use something that at least looked real," I said.

"Yeah, well," said Frodo. "He was working on having this mysto ring made using a real diamond. A red one, or a pink one, something like that. It was so we could like feel the power and attraction of beauty and money and yadda yadda yadda, but the jeweler crapped out on us."

"That must have made him really mad," I said, half convinced by this whole conversation that it was indeed Rodney who'd put Sylvia up to buying Chelsea's ring.

I went back and forth—it was a Rodney/Sylvia scheme, no it was a Tonio/Sylvia scheme. Heck, maybe they were all three in it together.

"Not at all, actually. Not having the ring made Rodney rethink the whole scene. He decided that it'd be better to make a statement about how we risk our lives for things that turn out to be worthless or meaningless. Something like that. You know, all that glitters is not gold. Now he's totally into the big fake stone. I heard him tell the art department guy that the stone didn't even look fake enough."

I couldn't believe this. "So he doesn't even care? He doesn't feel cheated, or ripped off, or . . . or . . ." The moment the words leaped from my mouth I could tell I sounded too concerned. I mean, why would the fate of Rodney von Lager's red diamond mean anything at all to me?

"Nah, he's over it," said Frodo.

But suddenly, I felt Tonio's eyes on me. I glanced over. He was staring at me, lips pursed, eyebrows pinched together over his big brown eyes. For the first time I could read his face. He was trying to put two and two together, and was winding up with five. Me. Chelsea. The ring Chelsea sold his sister. His sister missing. And now mention of Rodney's red diamond, which also for reasons that weren't common knowledge, also had disappeared. I stared right back at him.

Tonio and the actor playing Frodo—whose name turned out to be Dusty—sat down at the end of a long table covered with a white tablecloth. There was a spare folding chair next to them, so I sat down, too. Dusty snuck me a soda from the ice chest. They ignored me, talked about when they were getting paid, and how they were going to spend the money. Dusty mentioned a college fund and a new deck for his skateboard. Tonio said he was sending most of it to his grandma in Puerto Vallarta, for an operation she needed. He didn't know what it was.

At that moment, Rodney clapped his big hands and asked everyone to please listen up. He had an announcement regarding the schedule.

Tonio and Dusty stood up, dumped their paper plates. It was obviously time for me to take off.

Tonio said, "You'll let me know if you hear anything from Sylvia, won't you?" Was it my imagination, or was there a new intensity in his voice?

I lied. I said sure.

I rode home, wondering all the way whether you could collapse from sweating. Somehow it escaped me that since riding to Chelsea's house and then on to the skate park was all downhill, it would be all uphill on the return trip. I tied my hair in a knot on top of my head, but it was no use. The sweat ran down the sides of my face and into my eyes. It was now mid-afternoon, the hottest time of the day in Portland, which, as we learned in seventh-grade geography, is a northern city and thus gets its head-sweating heat later in the day than say, a city on the equator.

I stood up on the pedals, struggled and puffed. Mark Clark was right. I needed more exercise. I needed to play tennis or soccer or run around the block in a jogging outfit, like some of the people in our neighborhood. I was perishing of thirst. I thought how rude Tonio was not to offer me water on a day like this.

I avoided the street where the big, possum-eating hawk lived. I was sure he would register my red face, drenched T-shirt, and gasping for air as easy prey, pluck me off the bike, and claw my eyes out. I pedaled faster.

I was never more happy to see Casa Clark, sitting big and Mexican restaurant–like on its hilly corner. As I coasted into the driveway Morgan staggered out of the garage hugging his sleeping bag and tent to his chest. He was going on a camping trip to Eastern Oregon. I dropped the bike in the driveway and lunged for the garden hose. Morgan dumped his stuff next to the picnic table.

"Hey," said Morgan, "easy on the bike."

I gulped down as much metallic-tasting hose water as I could possibly hold before wiping my mouth and turning off the spigot. "The thing doesn't have a kickstand, Morgan, what do you expect me to do?"

Morgan laughed. "It's a mountain bike, they don't have kickstands."

I ignored him. I had more important things to do, like call Chelsea. I popped my Bluetooth around my ear and voice dialed Chelsea's number. She picked up on the first ring.

"You've got to get over here, now," I said. "Big developments. Remember that dude Tonio at Sylvia's apartment? Her little brother? He's in Rodney von Lager's new movie. And he's worried to death because his big sis hasn't been home for a few days—since around the time she bought the ring. I went to—"

Chelsea let out a big sigh, like air escaping from a balloon. "Minerva, I just can't."

"Can't what?"

"Whatever it is you want. Come over, get together, rehash this diamond thing. I played eighteen holes with my dad today. Eighteen holes. I'm dead."

"I think we're really close to figuring out who has the diamond." Well, not really, but *closer*, anyway. We had a lot more clues and a lot more suspects, that was for sure.

"My dad is going to try to have his insurance pay for it," said Chelsea. "That's what he told me today. So no worries."

"What do you mean? I thought because he was sneaking the diamond into the country there was no insurance on it?" I said.

"I don't know!" said Chelsea. "My dad'll work it out! I'm so exhausted. Right now I'm going down to the club with Mom to sit in the Jacuzzi. So, take it easy, all right?"

"Take it easy? What's with you? Someone stole like a million-dollar diamond right out from under your nose and you don't *care*?"

"I care," she said sleepily, "just not at this exact moment."

"That really sucks," I said.

"Oh Minerva, whatever." And then just like that she hung up on me.

We Clarks tend to be slow-burners. We don't fly off the handle. This is because our ancestors come from England and other places where it never pays to scream and throw a fit. I dialed Reggie. We'd been best friends since we were fetuses. He could stop thinking about Amanda the Panda for three seconds and help me figure out what I had here.

I expected it to go straight to voice mail, and nearly fainted with shock when he answered on the first ring.

"I really don't think you're being fair," said Reggie. His voice was so low I hardly recognized it.

Huh? He obviously thought I was Amanda the Panda, or someone else, anyway.

"Well, you know that life isn't fair," I said. "Your dad tells you that about every other day."

He was silent for a second. "Oh. Hi, Minerva."

"What's wrong with you?" I asked.

"What's going on?" he said, changing the subject.

"I need an IP. Meet me at the school in ten." Our school was five blocks away from my house and five blocks away from his house, exactly, and whenever we needed to have a real discussion, as opposed to a random time-wasting IM discussion (yes, yes, even I know that IMing is pointless), we met at the playground.

"Aw," said Reggie. "I can't. I'm kind of in the middle of something."

"I'll come over to your house then," I said.

"No you won't," said Mark Clark, who'd appeared from inside the house. He was carrying a black plastic bag full of garbage, which he dumped in the big can beside the garage. "You haven't done your chores from yesterday."

"I had basic electronics yesterday," I said to Mark Clark as he disappeared back into the house.

"You're taking basic electronics?" asked Reggie. This perked him up a little.

"Thank you, drive through please," I said. This was our private brush-off line. It meant "see if I tell you," or "I'm changing the subject," or "get *out*." We overused it, but it still cracked us up.

"Electronics are awesome," said Reggie. "You can blow stuff up."

I recounted the story of cranky Mr. Lawndale and

the exploding capacitors, and for a good thirty seconds I had my friend's undivided attention. "Could you meet me? Just for ten minutes?"

He hesitated. "Maybe later, how about?"

"It's that stupid Amanda the Panda, isn't it?" I said.

"Just—look, you totally don't get it, Minerva," he said.

"It?" I snapped. "What 'it' are you talking about? Being totally, stupidly obsessed with someone? Is that the 'it' you mean? Because if it is, I certainly do get it. So don't be insulting." My voice got loud and high. Morgan looked over from where he was fiddling with his tent.

"Oh, you mean that tall guy you were drooling all over at the dance?" said Reggie.

"I wasn't drooling on him. We were talking," I said.

"Is that what they call it now?" said Reggie.

"Why don't you ask The Panda," I said. "Since she runs your whole life these days." Why were we snapping at each other?

"Think I will. At least she's not a total biatch." Then he hung up on me.

What was going on with my friends? Chelsea was the one who had called *me*, begging for help. Reggie, who was normally interested in all sorts of strange things, and would certainly have loved to help me track down a missing jewel, had suddenly turned into a complete dimwit. If this was what being in love did to you, then I was so so so totally glad that Kevin was not calling me from Montana, like he'd promised. I checked my messages one more time, just to make sure he hadn't called—and he hadn't—good! I didn't want to become totally damaged like Reggie. I felt sorry for Reggie. And I felt sorry for myself, all of a sudden. Even though it was all working out for the best that Kevin was not my boyfriend, because he had not called me, I still wished he had, so that I could not return the call.

I sat down heavily on the picnic table. How did anyone ever have a boyfriend without going totally mad?

I wound up telling Morgan everything, not about Kevin, but about the missing red diamond. I didn't mean to, but I was stressed. I am not a drama queen, not usually. He listened while he pulled his tent out of its carrying sack and examined the seams, counted the poles.

I began not at the beginning, but with the de Guzmans' big house with the pillars, their all-white kitchen, and Mrs. de Guzman, who seemed so lonely. I told about how they kept three champion corgis who had their own dog nanny, and how they traveled all over the world (the de Guzmans, not the corgis) for Mr. de Guzman's jewelry business. I told how Mr. de Guzman just brought back a red diamond, small but rare, from London for Rodney von Lager.

Morgan has most of Rodney von Lager's movies on DVD. He was a fan before Rodney was famous, when he still worked in advertising and made his weird little black-and-white shorts in his free time. Morgan knew all about Rodney's perfectionism, and had also heard the story about the time and money he spent to put the window in the closet that no one would ever see.

Still, when I said that I thought Rodney von Lager stole the diamond, Morgan shook his head. "Nah," he said, "I don't think so."

"But he knew when Mr. de Guzman was bringing in the diamond. And a rare red diamond is worth a lot of money. It would save him money on his movie."

"True, but it doesn't make sense. Rodney is richer than God. He's been nominated for an Oscar, people pay him a lot. He doesn't need to steal anything."

"Maybe he did it just for the fun of it, just to see if he could do it or something," I said. Rodney was looking less guilty by the second.

"Maybe," said Morgan. He folded his tent back up and slid it into the carrying bag. "But how come the guy you said was playing Frodo didn't have it? They were filming today. It wasn't rehearsal. If he'd stolen the diamond, you would have seen it in the ring. They wouldn't be using a fake."

I told him about how Rodney was now into the big fake stone and making an ironic statement about how we risk our lives for things that turn out to be worthless, blah blah blah.

Morgan said, "That really proves the point. The red

diamond was probably just sort of a whim. You know, Hollywood people are like that."

I sighed, sat down right there on the driveway, stuck my legs straight out in front of me. The concrete was cool beneath my thighs. Morgan had a point. Morgan always had a point. Morgan is possibly my most brilliant brother, even though he is the youngest and the quietest.

"You know what the worst thing is?" I said. "I feel as if I'm all alone. Chelsea de Guzman wasn't even my friend, but she called me all desperate begging me to help her. So I said sure, and I'm trying my best, and now she's like, 'I'm too tired because I went golfing' and 'no worries because my dad says his insurance is going to take care of it.' Isn't she, like, curious?"

Morgan laughed a little. He took off his earflap hat and tossed it on the picnic table. I wasn't used to seeing him without his hat, which he wore, he said, to keep as much hair on his head as possible. He was already going bald, Morgan was.

"She's probably just not curious, Min. I would say most people you'll come across on this planet are not curious."

"Then why did she call me?"

"Because her butt was in a sling with her dad. At least, in the beginning. Now you say he says he's figured out a way to recoup his money. It's not as compelling to her anymore."

"But I still care. I still want to find out what happened to the diamond. And why should I? It has nothing to do with me, but I still care!"

Morgan sat down right next to me on the driveway. The sun had dropped behind the other side of the house. We sat in the cool shadow.

"Do you know what my major is?" asked Morgan.

"In college? You want to be either a lawyer like Dad or a spoken word poet, last I heard."

"My major is philosophy, though. The main purpose of being a philosophy major is to learn how to think and how to solve problems. But people laugh at me. They make the same ridiculous jokes about it all the time. 'So, you going to get a job at IBM as a professional philosopher? Ho ho ho.'"

I didn't say anything. Morgan sometimes takes awhile to get to the point. "What that always says to me is that people no longer value thinking about things, or solving problems, if they ever did. But I like thinking about stuff. I like solving problems. I think it's valuable and interesting, just because."

"Just because?" I said. "Is that like the quote I heard one time about why mountain climbers climb mountains? Just because they're there?"

"Pretty much."

"So maybe I want to solve this mystery because I'm just plain old curious?"

"Yep. Except there's nothing plain about genuine curiosity. It's one of the rarest things around."

"As rare as a red diamond?" I asked

"Yep."

We sat without saying anything for a long minute. It was seven o'clock. Through the kitchen window I could see Mark Clark moving, probably starting dinner. Suddenly, I was starving. I hoped dinner involved cheese and bread, my two favorite food groups.

"And hey," said Morgan. "I know you probably hear this from enough people, but be careful. Don't do anything stupid, okay?"

"I won't," I said. But I didn't promise.

- 9 -

The next morning, Monday, I woke up depressed even though my room was bright with sun. Kevin hadn't called and I knew somehow that he never would. Mark Clark and Quills were at work. Morgan had left that morning for Eastern Oregon, camping with some of his philosopher friends from college. Dad was on an airplane over North Dakota or in a New York City courtroom, somewhere or other. Mom was coming home on Sunday. She had big plans for togetherness: shopping, zucchini bread–baking, mother-daughter yoga. It seemed pretty unlikely that I would solve the mystery of the missing red diamond before the weekend.

Morgan was right. If Rodney von Lager had begun filming his movie with a completely different stone, he probably hadn't stolen the diamond. Tonio was still a suspect, but just barely. He didn't know where his sister was, and my guess was that wherever she was, the diamond was with her. That left Shark, Sylvia's security guard boyfriend, who, according to Tonio, volunteered at the humane society in order to pick up girls. Even though Tonio didn't like him, I thought maybe he might know something, or spill a clue or two.

I knew all about the Portland Humane Society. I'd never visited, but a lot of eighth graders at our school volunteered there. It sat on a long leg of industrial highway near the Columbia River, which forms the border between Oregon and Washington. Its neighbors are a steelyard, a factory that makes truck parts, a heavy equipment rental place, and some plain low buildings that sell weird stuff like welding supplies, garage doors, and huge truck tires. On the corner is a greasy spoon named Patsy's, which looks like somewhere you'd go if you wanted to get robbed in the ladies' room.

I took the bus. I was worried that the humane society would be as sad and desolate as everything else on this run-down boulevard, surrounded by a chain-link fence topped with razor wire that shone in the sun. "Desolate" was one of our seventh-grade spelling words, and here I was using it in my own head. I chewed my thumb cuticle. I imagined that a shelter for pets no one wanted would be a sad place, with rows of cages filled with lonely dogs and cats curled in their corners, depressed.

My spirits lifted when the bus stopped near an almost brand-new building, cream-colored with teal blue trim and a red roof. Outside, it looked like a library. Inside, there were plenty of clean windows, a big clean lobby with a cool design on the gleaming linoleum, and a gift shop filled with fleece dog jackets, leopard-print cat beds, pink leather-studded dog collars, organic treats and fancy curry combs, doggie greeting cards and key chains, kitty cat posters and calendars.

It was so cheery, I allowed myself to forget for a moment that I wasn't there to visit the cats in their cat condos in Kitty Village, behind a big glass window just off the lobby, or to pick out a puppy. The Help Desk was sleek and curved, made of some pale wood. A bunch of fat orange roses sat in a glass vase on one corner. No one was behind the desk. Two ladies in baggy shorts and white running shoes peered into Kitty Village, scratching the glass and cooing. They didn't notice me at all.

I wandered around, looked in the small pets section to see if they had any ferrets, read a wall plaque that talked about the history of the humane society. It's the oldest one in the west. I kept waiting for Shark or somebody to show up at the front desk. I asked the man working in the gift shop, a grandpa type with half glasses on a chain around his neck, and he said they were probably tending to something in the Dog Pod. He nodded his head in the direction of a pair of glass double doors. On the wall behind the doors was a big banner that had a grinning beagle mix and the words: COME FIND YOUR NEW BEST FRIEND!

That got to me. I needed a new best friend. Chelsea de Guzman only called because she was in trouble at that moment, and Reggie was too busy with Amanda the Panda. And Kevin? I won't even go there.

Now, I had Jupiter of course, whom I love as much as a human can love a ferret, but he didn't feel like my best friend so much as a cool little kid I'd been hired to babysit, who was always getting into things. He never jumped into my arms the way Ned did that one day on the de Guzmans' front lawn.

I walked through the doors and into the first group of kennels, or pods, where I tried not to spend too much time bonding with Dory, the black and white Lab mix, or Buckwheat, the tricolor pit bull/chow chow mix, or Maury the blind-in-one-eye border collie. I wanted them all.

At the end of the row of kennels, along the back wall, were the puppies, most of them asleep in a heap. There were notices posted on the front of their kennels; most of them were already spoken for. Beside the puppy kennels an emergency exit stood propped open with a chair.

Out back, it was something else altogether. Past a row of covered play areas, where people who wanted to adopt a dog got to hang out with him a little, was a trio of blue Dumpsters, locked neatly behind a chain-link fence with a shiny lock. Past them, through an opening in another chain-link fence, it was pure urban wilderness: a huge, sloping junkyard that was home to piles of rusty car parts, construction debris, a mini forest of thorny blackberry canes, and a strange structure that looked like nothing I'd ever seen before.

I left the shelter, walked through the opening in the fence, stepped with care through some broken glass and weeds to get closer. It was a large white water tank tipped on its side, with a big cage made of chicken wire attached to it.

At the exact moment I got close enough to figure out what it was, I heard *gruhu gruhu gruhu,* and a half-dozen white pigeons strutted out through a square hole in the tank wall into the cage. Ugh, birds! I leaped back, practically falling onto a rusty car axle. Into my blood system poured all those fear chemicals we learned about in science. I hopped around, shook my arms, trying to fling off the bird cooties. What was a pigeon coop doing back here? Were these pigeons up for adoption, too, but they were so scary and disgusting, they had to be kept all the way out here?

I jogged back to the half-open emergency exit door, wondering why the emergency exit was open in the first place, when I heard a man's gruff voice. The voice came from behind me, across the garbage-strewn lot. I couldn't hear what he said, just the nasty tone.

I turned around and saw two storage sheds on the other side of the empty lot. The man had just locked one of the sheds and was coming toward me, carrying what looked to be a Frisbee.

It was Sylvia's boyfriend, Shark. I recognized the slope of his shoulders, the beaky nose. I didn't think he'd seen me. He was looking down, watching where he walked, stepping over a broken hump of something white and gleaming, perhaps a toilet.

This gave me time to duck back inside the shelter, jog past the puppies, who were awake now, wrestling and squealing, back through the Dog Pod, past Dory, Buck-wheat, and Maury, the blind-in-one eye border collie who was busy chasing his own tail, through the glass double doors.

Just as I reentered the lobby, my gaze fell upon a rack of forms, hanging on a post beneath the words "Volunteer Applications." I grabbed one and went to the front desk, where I bent my head and nibbled on my bottom lip in deep thought, as if I'd been working on filling this out for fifteen minutes.

I should say right here that the moment I plucked the application from the rack, I started thinking that volunteering here might solve a few problems. After basic electronics was over Mark Clark would be on me again about finding something to do with my summer. Also, my school requires that all eighth graders perform twenty hours of community service in order to graduate. I always thought that community service was something minor criminals were sentenced to instead of jail, but I guess it also goes for kids who go to Catholic school.

I read over the first paragraph of the application eight hundred times. Junior volunteers were twelve to fifteen and their main duties included cleaning cages, walking dogs, and playing with cats.

"Hey hey hey, if it isn't Tonio's little lady friend! Suzanne, right?"

I looked up from the form as if I'd been in deep concentration. It was Shark. He wasn't wearing his security guard uniform, obviously, but a long-sleeved moss green T-shirt with PORTLAND HUMANE SOCIETY stitched over the pocket in gold and a pair of faded straight-leg Levi's. His pants were too short. I could see plenty of white sweat sock above his sneakers. I pretended not to recognize him, and my blank expression must have done the trick, because he chuckled at himself.

"Guess all us grown-ups look alike, huh."

"Pardon?" I said.

He narrowed his long pale eyes a little, took the measure of me as sure as if he was reading a thermometer. I guess he decided it best not to remind me where he knew me from.

"What can I do for you today?"

"I wanted to volunteer," I said.

"Can I . . ." He made a pinching motion with his fingers. His hands were small for someone his size. I passed him the form. He barely glanced at it. "We're not accepting any volunteers at the moment, but I'll be sure to contact you if we do."

"Are you in charge of the volunteer program then?"

"There are no openings now, Suzanne. But maybe you might like to adopt a pet? We have some new pups. Have you checked out our Dog Pod?"

I said I hadn't. It seemed like a good idea not to let on that I'd already been to the dog adoption center, where I might have peeked through the emergency exit and seen Shark tromping through the junky lot with his Frisbee.

At home I let Jupiter out of his cage and he bounced off the legs of the sofa, flipped and rolled, making that dooking sound ferrets make when they're full of joy. He was so happy to be out of his cage. Guilt swarmed over me; I had not played with Jupiter in weeks. I found one of his favorite toys—an old flip-flop—and sat on the bottom stair watching him drag it down the hallway. He held it close to his chest with his little paws and scooted backwards, every once in awhile running into the wall with his skinny ferret rear end.

Normally, this would make me sob with laughter, but

I just sat in thinker pose, my chin resting on my fist. The morning had been a pure waste of time, and I was mad at myself for not reminding Shark that I'd run into him at Sylvia's apartment, and asking whether or not he'd talked to Sylvia lately. That had been the whole point of going to the humane society, hadn't it?

Yet something stopped me from talking to Shark. Tonio was right. He was nice, but it was phony. Shark was a little creepy.

Just as Jupiter ran into the front door at the end of the hall, my cell rang: Chelsea.

"I just wanted to say I'm sooooooo sorry about yesterday. I was just really exhausted. I'm the type of person who takes a long time to get over jet lag. That's what my mom's naturopath said."

"It's okay," I said.

"Really. I'm really really sorry. My mom said you came over and hung out with her and everything. She thinks you're really a cool girl."

"I had a good time. She told me the diamond was for Rodney von Lager," I said.

"Who?"

"The filmmaker?"

"I just thought it was for some rich West Hills lady or something," she said. "Maybe he stole it!"

I caught her up on everything. Told her about going to the set down at the skate park, and running into the boy Tonio, who it turned out was one of the costars of Rodney's new movie.

"That kid's in a movie? Luck-y! I want to be in a movie." She made her voice fake pouty. "How do I get to be in a movie?"

I then told her about running into Shark, how I found him alone in Sylvia's apartment that day, and how there was something weird about the guy. I told her about taking the bus out to the humane society and filling out an application to volunteer.

"Ugh. Why would you do that? The place smells like pet pee."

"Actually, it's pretty nice. They have a new building. Inside, it reminds you of being in a library."

"Well, I've never been there."

"I just can't help feeling that there's something else happening out there. Shark is . . . I don't know . . . up to something."

"Was he like totally a suspicious character?" asked Chelsea. "And what's with that name. Shark? Who names their kid Shark?"

"I don't know. It was on the patch over his pocket, on his uniform."

"Was he scary then?"

"Not at all. Phony nice. Bland as bundt cake."

"Bland as bundt cake?" screeched Chelsea. "Who says *that*?"

"I don't know," I said. "Nobody." Of course, my mom said that. My mom, who was coming home in six days and counting. She'd left a phone message while I was wasting the day at the humane society asking if I still liked to do jigsaw puzzles.

"So, you want to go to Urban Outfitters? My mom could drive us. They're having a sale on their printed tees. They have a totally adorable one with a pink dove on it."

"I don't think so. I've got some stuff I'm supposed to do."

"Maybe when I get back you can come over and I can French braid your hair. Has anyone ever French braided your hair? We could do a CD swap. You could spend the night maybe."

"Maybe," I said. I got the feeling Chelsea was trying to make it up to me for being so snippy the day before. That was okay, though. I wouldn't mind going to Urban Outfitters and having my hair French braided and do-ing a CD swap, but we were in the middle of trying to solve this mystery, you know?

"Are doves and pigeons the same thing?" I asked.

"What?"

"Are doves the same thing as pigeons?" I suddenly could not get my mind off that strange water tank pi-geon coop behind the shelter. What was it doing there?

Chelsea sighed loudly. "You know, Minerva, you really

are bizarre. I mean, I gotta tell you, you were weird before you had that accident or whatever, but now you've gone complete nut job."

"I know that," I said. I'd come to realize that my accident had changed me from not normal in one way to not normal in another.

"I mean, it's not like you're fugly. In fact, my mom said you were the kind of girl who would one day turn out to be a beautiful *woman,* but jeez Minerva, get yourself some skirts, fix your hair, get it together."

"I have it together," I said. "That's part of the trouble. Most girls our age don't have anything together. All they think about are their clothes and hair."

"That's what we're supposed to think about, Minerva. Not doves and pigeons, or whatever it is you're obsessing about. I'm just trying to be nice to you. I'm trying to like be your friend, all right? I could be asking Hannah or Julia or any one of those girls to hang out, but I'm not. I'm asking you, because you've like tried to help me out, but you are just not normal."

Then she hung up on me.

That night I had a bird nightmare. It was hot in my room. The sheets got all twisted around my legs. Mark Clark had made burritos for dinner, and had put extra red pepper flakes in the ground beef, and I think that might have accounted for the bad dream, where pigeons were flying around inside my room, hundreds of them.

They opened my drawers, pulled out all my T-shirts and cutoffs, pecked at the keys of my computer. They didn't land on me at all, but in the dream there was the impending sense that after they ruined all my things, they would come after me. I kept waiting for someone to open my bedroom door and shoo the birds away, but no one ever did.

The next morning Mark Clark gave me a list of chores before he went to work. "The house needs some sprucing up before Mom gets here," he said.

"Why?" I said. "We're out of Cap'n Crunch, too." I sat at the breakfast table eating the last of the Frosted Mini-Wheats, the awful guinea pig shavings at the bottom of the box. With nonfat milk. Mark Clark tucked the chore list under my elbow. I took my cell out of my pocket, turned it on, and saw I had voice mail. My heart just about hopped out of my mouth. Kevin?

No, Reggie. He must have called while I was talking to Chelsea the night before.

"Hi Minerva, it's Reg. Please call when you can." His voice sounded all flat and weird, like he was POed at me. I called him back, but it went straight to voice mail. Before I could leave a message, Mark Clark picked up his chore list and held it in front of my face.

"Are you paying attention to me?"

"Yeah." I slid my phone back in my pocket.

Quills was hunkered down over his three-egg-white omelet. Mark Clark frowned. "What did you do with the yolks?"

"And away goes trouble, down the drain," Quills sang without looking up. He was reading the funnies. He looked up, drummed his chin with his pointer finger and asked, "Why do they call them funnies when they're not even funny, I wonder."

Mark Clark cranked open the dining room windows. It was already warm, even though it wasn't even nine o'clock. A yellow jacket flew into the room. We Clarks don't scream and jump around at the sight of insects, even stinging ones.

"I'd like you to edit the fridge," said Mark Clark.

I looked up. Was he talking to me? Quills sprinkled more pepper on his omelet.

"I just cleaned the refrigerator," I said.

"We should get rid of the cookie dough and that box of wine," said Mark Clark.

Quills snorted. "I don't see why."

"Mom called this morning. Rolando's coming with her, I guess."

Quills snorted. "Oh man, not *him*. I'm not editing the fridge for that dude."

Talk about the mystery of love and attraction! Rolando was Mom's hippie boyfriend. He was nice enough, I guess. Mom said he was "very caring, very present," which I took to mean he wasn't always out of town on business, like our dad. The biggest problem with Rolando was—he had a braid! Down the middle of his back! How could my mom be in love with someone with a man braid?

Rolando also turned our mom to the dark side of eating. She now ate organic everything and didn't believe in processed food or anything that wasn't free range. She'd become a freak about it. Mom was all about finding your bliss, unless it happened to include keeping a junk food drawer stocked with Flamin' Hot Cheetos and pork rinds.

Mark Clark sighed and sat down at the head of the table with his bagel and crossword puzzle. No one said anything. Outside, someone was mowing the lawn. Poor Mark Clark. I tried not to think about his life too much. Unlike Quills and Morgan, who always seemed to be going snowboarding or Jet Skiing or breaking up with some new crazy girlfriend, or who got on airplanes and went to Los Angeles (Quills) or Kuala Lumpur (Morgan), Mark Clark went to work at his computer network security job, and came home and played on his computer, and went to bed. He paid the bills and made sure we had milk and laundry detergent.

After Mark Clark and Quills went to work I got rid of the stuff in the fridge Mom would make a fuss over. It didn't seem fair for Mark Clark to get lectured about what we ate when he was only the older brother, and not the parent.

I took a shower and washed my hair, even though I don't like taking a shower when no one else is in the house. I didn't comb my hair—which made it frizzy big and stranger than it already was—but pressed it between both palms with a dry towel. It dried wavy curly that way. Some gel made it shine.

It wasn't even noon and I was bored out of my skull.

As if my cell phone could feel my ennui—the French word for boredom; I know it because Quills's band is working on a new song called "Ennui on Wheels"—it vibrated inside my back pocket.

I didn't even allow myself to hope that it would be Kevin.

I popped on my Bluetooth over my ear.

It was Shark, from the humane society, telling me they did need a volunteer after all, and could I come right over?

I did not hurry right over, though. I needed to wait for my hair to dry, and I needed to think. I pulled on a pair of jeans and my good luck Green Day T-shirt, which I got at the concert, which was the first concert I'd *ever* been to. It said **I ♥ GD**—I love Green Day—but instead of a regular heart it was a heart-shaped hand grenade. Cool, huh? I gave my teeth a quick brush, stuck my phone in one front pocket, my Bluetooth in the other.

I had not believed Shark yesterday when he said they didn't need volunteers. At the end of seventh grade, when Ms. Kettle, our religion teacher, told us about the required twenty service hours of community service, she said that if we could not find anywhere else to put in our time, the humane society always needed people to change the kitty litter and play with the dogs, who were always in danger of becoming depressed out of loneliness.

For some reason, Shark had wanted me to leave, and now he wanted me to come back.

Even though it was sunny and warm, I put on my white hoodie with the blue Hawaiian flowers running down one arm, opened Jupiter's cage, scooped him up from where he was sleeping, curled like the letter C in his hammock, and set off.

A grown-up would have told me it was a dumb idea to take my own pet to the humane society, but I had a feeling I was going to need some help.

I stepped off the bus and the doors sighed closed behind me. The bus didn't stop directly in front of the shelter, but near the far end of the parking lot, which wrapped around the side of the building, before becoming the junkyard urban wilderness lot. From where I stood I couldn't see the pigeon coop, nor most of the larger piles of automotive parts, but I could see part of the front of the shed, hidden behind some shrubs.

The bus eased away behind me, leaving me standing alone on the hot sidewalk, no one around, only a few trucks moseying down the highway in the heat. I could glimpse part of the shed, at the back of the lot. I knew from having glimpsed it the day before that it was small, and made of unfinished wood that had turned a silvery gray, as unpainted wood always did in our climate. It didn't look like a cute little barn or chalet, like some of the sheds in the backyards of our neighbors. There were no windows, and even from where I stood I could see that the door didn't hang right on its hinges. It was so plain you could easily get used to it being there and not even see it.

Suddenly, the door of the shed opened. I thrust my hands into my hoodie pocket and around Jupiter's thin furry body, just out of I don't know what.

Shark came out of the shed, turned, said a few words, then closed the door and locked it. He was carrying the same Frisbee I'd seen the day before, only now, balanced in the middle of it, I could see a white coffee cup, a speck of green in the center. It was from Starbucks. And the Frisbee wasn't a Frisbee at all, but a dinner plate.

I waited until I thought Shark went back inside, then quickly walked through the parking lot. Even though I was sweating like a shy boy at a dance, I was glad I wore my hoodie. As I waded through the mini forest of weeds and homely overgrown shrubs, blackberry canes seemed to leap up out of nowhere and snag my sleeves and pants legs. For those few yards, I could have used a machete.

The shed was old, built on a low foundation. There were two rickety steps up. I knocked on the door softly. "Hello? Anybody home?" Anybody *home?* That was a brilliant thing to say.

I could swear I heard someone breathing, but it could have been my own breath. I was afraid to say anything else, for fear my beating heart would leap out of my mouth, sprout legs, and run off. I knocked again. Nothing. Just as I started to think I was wrong, that no one was in the shed, that maybe this was just Shark's private place where he ate his lunch . . . no, impossible . . . no one would come out here to relax . . . ever . . . another idea bloomed: What if whoever was in there was bound and gagged?

I looked behind me and far off, across the lot, I could see the emergency exit propped open with a chair, just as it had been the day before. Every once in awhile I could hear a dog bark. Car parts glinted in the sun. Flies and who knows what other stinging creatures buzzed around. Jupiter squirmed in my pocket.

I couldn't stand there forever. As long as the emergency exit was open, anyone—including Shark—could see me.

The door to the shed was locked from the outside with a big rusty slide bolt. I looked again at the crookedly hung door. Along the bottom there was a small gap, maybe two inches? I never knew how people could look at the size of a space and know how big it was; maybe it was the same as how as you got older, you got better at doing arithmetic in your head.

Anyway, all I knew was that it was ferret-sized.

I poured Jupiter out of my pocket, whispered in his tiny ear that this was even better than crawling around inside the kitchen cabinets, and fed him through the gap. I put my ear to the door and heard what I'd expected: muffled struggling and shrieking, i.e., someone freaking out at what they probably thought was a rat or an opossum.

All right.

Now what?

I flipped open my cell phone. I had to call someone, some adult who would know what to do. The obvious choice would be the police, except the police didn't believe me. I thought back on all the stupid calls I'd made about the guy in the knit cap, who went through our trash cans on garbage day looking for bottles to recycle, and about the house next door getting TPed. I felt myself blush with the ridiculousness of it. I was a modern girl who cried wolf. I could just imagine the deep, amused-sounding voice of the 911 operator, the one who always answered when she recognized my number, the one who thought I was a kick in the pants, telling me I needed to stop pestering them.

But this was a real emergency.

As I stood there wondering whether I should call anyway, the phone began vibrating in my hand. I saw it was Chelsea.

"Guess what I did today?" she sang.

I moved off the steps and crouched down among the blackberries and broken bottles. "Make it quick," I whispered, "something's going on here, too."

"Just guess."

"Just *tell* me," I practically shouted. Chelsea de Guzman could give you PMS no matter the time of month. Jeez.

"I felt so bad about when we talked yesterday, and was feeling so much better this morning, completely un-jet lagged, I decided to come out to the humane society to check things out. You said something was up out there, so I thought I'd pitch in. My mom is always saying I don't pitch in enough. Plus, I thought we could volunteer together, get our community service hours out of the way.

"So I come in—you're right, it's a very cool place— and who's sitting behind the counter but Frank, our dog nanny. So I go, 'Frankie! What are you doing here!'"

"Your dog sitter works at the humane society?"

"He volunteers, I guess, when he isn't taking care of Winkin', Blinkin', and Ned."

Was this possible? That Sylvia's boyfriend Shark *and* the de Guzmans' dog sitter Frank worked here together? "When did you come in?"

"This morning. First thing." She sounded proud of herself. "Frankie is just the sweetest guy."

"Was anyone else working with him?"

"Nobody that I saw. It was early."

"You didn't tell him that the diamond had been stolen, did you?"

"Well, I did! I told him the whole story, about that Sylvia chick buying the ring off of me, and how we went to her apartment and found the ring but not the diamond. He said that he would do everything he could to help us. He said that when you came to the humane society yesterday, you shouldn't have pretended that you didn't know him, that that was dumb because he recognized you right off the bat . . ."

My stomach felt as if it was about to drop out of my body.

"Chelsea. Why did he say that? I've never met Frank. Where did he say he recognized me from?"

There was a long silence. I had the worst feeling about this.

"He didn't say . . . oh *no!*" she said. "I just thought of something. Oh, this could be *bad.*"

"What?"

"Frank's last name is Sharkey."

"So he might also go by Shark?" I said.

"Which would make them the same guy."

I opened my mouth to tell her that I was at the humane society that very moment, but before I could formulate a sentence I heard hasty footsteps, rustling, swearing, then looked up to see Frank/Shark swoop down on me, yank the cell phone out of my hand, snap it shut, and throw it into the bushes. He reminded me of a cobra, suddenly, with his cold squinty eyes, stooped shoulders, and smile that bordered on a sneer.

He grabbed my upper arm hard enough to break it, dragged me to the door of the shed, unlocked the lock, and hurled me inside. It happened so fast I hardly had time to be scared. Frank/Shark wasn't so nice anymore. His face was red, his green eyes squinty slits. He looked as if he could snap my neck and go straight back to cuddling puppies without missing a beat.

- 10 -

A girl who could only be Sylvia Soto sat on a bench in the corner. The bench was a wide shelf built into the wall. An ancient, dirty sleeping bag with what looked like a red plaid lining was spread beneath her legs. She wore a flowered cotton skirt, dirty pink flip-flops, and an oversized sweatshirt, black or dark blue, I couldn't tell in the gloom. I'd guessed that Frank—Shark, I mean, and what a lame nickname may I just say?—had given her the sweatshirt for when it got cold at night. She had a few pieces of duct tape slapped across the bottom half of her face. She had enormous eyes and that dark hair like a horse tail, which Chelsea had re-marked upon.

Frank threw me on a narrow wooden chair and tied my hands behind it with a length of white plastic rope.

On a Scale of Scared between one and ten, I was at a seven. This meant I was afraid, but not totally pants-peeing out of my mind terrified. Part of the reason was that Sylvia didn't look out of her mind terrified, but rather so irritated I wouldn't have been surprised if steam started shooting out of her ears.

While Frank tied me up, and slapped a few lengths of duct tape over my mouth, he hissed at me through his teeth. "If you weren't sticking your nose in other people's business I wouldn't have had to do this, Suzanne. I'm a good guy, ask anybody, but when people get in the way of business, I lose my sense of humor."

At this, Sylvia rolled her enormous eyes. I was beginning to think Frank/Shark was nuts. People say other people are crazy all the time, and I always wondered what crazy looked like for real and not on television. This was it.

"This is all your fault," he said, looking at Sylvia. "If you had just let me handle this, you wouldn't be in this position." Then he heaved a big sigh, as if we were both unruly children it pained him to punish.

He turned to go, then spied Jupiter hissing in the corner. Poor Jupiter was up to ten on the Scale of Scared. I could tell because his tail was puffed out like a bottle brush. I didn't like this. I didn't like this at all. Seeing Jupiter upset and afraid made my throat close up. What if Frank tossed Jupiter into the bushes, the way he had my cell phone? Jupiter was smart, but he knew nothing about surviving in a junkyard urban wilderness. I squeezed my eyes shut, tried to erase the mental image of Jupiter being carried off by the hungry neighborhood hawk.

"What the . . . ?" said Frank, frowning.

He leaned closer, peered at Jupiter. Then, his face relaxed; his narrow-eyed lizardy expression vanished. "How'd you get in here, little guy?" He scooped Jupiter up. He was gentle. He balanced Jupiter on his muscular forearm, and began to pet him with great feeling. I noticed Frank had a tattoo encircling his wrist like a bracelet: BORN TO KICK BUTT. Oh, man, what a creepy dude.

Suddenly, it was as if Sylvia and I weren't there at all. Frank left with Jupiter. We heard the rusty bolt slide closed, then the crunch of his footsteps as he stomped back to the shelter.

I pushed the thought of what would happen to Jupiter out of my mind. I had to. It was dark and stuffy in the shed. It smelled damp and rodenty. The only fresh air came from the opening beneath the door, where Jupiter had snuck inside. Thin threads of light streamed through from cracks in the corners and ceiling.

Still, I wasn't too worried. I knew we'd be out of there soon.

You have probably heard of Bad Guy Aim. That's where, in every action movie, the bad guy suddenly forgets how to shoot and can't hit a thing. There is also such a thing as Bad Guy Knot Tying.

Over the years, my brothers and I have tied each other to chairs, doorknobs, piano legs, handrails, tree trunks, wrought iron fences, flagpoles, you name it. We used string, twine, yarn from our mom's knitting box, nylon rope, a blue and white rope Morgan used for rock climbing. Because I was the youngest, I got tied up the most, had the most opportunity to practice, and became the best Most Awesome Escape Artist in the entire Clark family.

From the feel of it, Frank had Bad Guy Knot Tying skills. He had secured my hands behind my back with a double overhand knot, but it hardly mattered. He was so intent on making sure my wrists were snug and the rope was tight, he forgot to tie me to the chair.

So I stood up, lifting my arms up over the chair back. Then I sat on the dusty floor, pulled my legs as close to my chest as possible, then scooched my arms beneath my rear. Once my hands were in front of me I could pull the tape off my mouth, and untie the rope with my teeth. I was free in a matter of minutes. I peeled the duct tape from my mouth—ouch—then, I untied Sylvia.

The first thing she did was scream, *"Help! Help us!"*

"Shhhhhhhhhhh!" I said. "Be quiet! You want him to come back and tie us up so we can't get free?" I sat next to her on her bench/bed. She was beautiful and exotic, with her coarse straight hair and strange almond-shaped gray eyes. In third grade I did a report on the Aztecs, and Sylvia possessed the same proud, high cheekboned face. She smelled sour, though. She'd probably been in there for days.

"Who in the hell are you anyway?" Sylvia had

"A friend of the girl whose diamond you stole."

"That stuck-up little rich girl sold me her ring fair and square. Oh God, how are we going to get out of here? You don't want to see Frank when his temper goes. Esta loco." She stood up, stretched her arms. "Now what? Any more bright ideas, little girl?"

"Tell me what you did with the diamond."

"Wow, aren't you a smarty-pants."

"Look, we don't have time for this. I can get us out of here, but I need to know some things first."

"How can you get us out of here?"

"I'm not telling, until you tell me some things."

"Oh, God! Between you and Frank, making everything my fault all the time. It's not my fault. This is not my fault."

"I never said it was, and I don't think it is. That Frank guy is obviously a wacko."

"He's my boyfriend," she sniffed. "We were supposed to get married this fall, on the autumnal equinox."

"Is that what the diamond was for?"

"God, no. How stupid do you think I am?" Sylvia

started to cry. She wept into her hands. I spied a thread of grit beneath each short nail. She told me the whole story. She met Frank at the shelter when she and Tonio came to adopt Chichi, the black pug. Frank had been so kind and helpful. Sylvia and Tonio were orphans, basically. Their father died in a car accident and as soon as Sylvia turned twenty-one their mother moved back to Puerto Vallarta to take care of her mother, Sylvia and Tonio's grandmother, who had diabetes. Sylvia sent most of the money she made cleaning hotel rooms home to Puerto Vallarta. Frank was a good man, she'd thought. He was so friendly and he loved animals. He also worked for a rich family, the de Guzmans, walking their show dogs.

"Frank got tired of seeing how much people spent on their pets. It was disgusting. Then, he overheard that de Guzman guy talking to his business partner about getting a red diamond for a movie director, the same movie director, Rodney Somebody, who had hired Tonio to play a part in his movie. Imagine, using a real diamond as a prop for a movie. How wasteful, how *sinful* is that? Frank and me, we were disgusted. Frank keeps his ears open. De Guzman talks openly in front of him like he is a piece of the furniture. But Frank is listening, all the time he is listening. It's not just any diamond de Guzman is bringing, it's a red diamond and it's worth a lot of money. Even split three ways, it is a lot of money. I could get my abuela better medical care, pay off my bills, set some aside for Tonio." She folded her arms.

"So Frank found out how Mr. de Guzman was bringing the diamond into the country, and sent you to the airport to buy the ring from Chelsea?"

"Frank had ideas about waiting until she was alone and mugging her, but I thought this was a cleaner way. Frank thinks he's like this bad guy—security guard by day, genius jewel thief by night! I knew buying the ring from the girl would work. I love jewelry myself. I remember being a young girl, and how flattered I felt when an older girl liked a necklace or bracelet I was wearing. That rich girl was no different. She would have given me that silly ring if I'd have kept up with the compliments."

I chewed my thumb cuticle, bounced my legs, tried to process this as fast as I could. I had to get to the bottom of everything, and it had to be soon. I had no idea how much time had passed.

"You said the money was going to be split three ways. You and Frank are only two."

"I don't know why I'm telling you all this. For all I know, Frank stuck you in here on purpose to find out where the diamond is. You got yourself untied pretty quick like. How do I know it's not a setup? That's something he would do. He thinks he's such an operator."

I told her about going to the airport and digging

through the garbage at Coffee People to find the receipt that had her drink order and name on it. "You ordered a Double Tall Caramel Soy Extra Foamy Latte."

"I could say that Frankie fed you that information, but he never gets it right. I been drinking plain double tall caramel lattes all week. He never listens to a thing I say. He's one of those guys who's all into you until he's got you, then he doesn't even pretend to be listening."

She ragged on Frank a bit more, how he treated her like she was the hired help, how he was jealous of every guy she said hello to while flirting madly with any woman who would look his way, how he lectured her, and now this, this, tying her up in a shed when she wouldn't bend to his will. "My question to myself always is, why am I with this guy? Why do I love a man who is so horrible?"

I could have told her that it was just the mystery of love and attraction, but I was determined not to get off topic.

"So who's got the diamond—you?" I held my breath. It couldn't possibly be this easy. She couldn't possibly have the diamond on her.

"Maybe."

"Where is it?"

She laughed and tossed her hair over her shoulder.

"Who's the third person?"

"You show me how you're going to get us out of

here." She motioned toward the door with her pointy chin. Sylvia had one of those heart-shaped faces they always call perfect in the beauty magazines, but it was marred by her surly expression.

I laughed. I said sure. I was convinced this mystery was almost solved. As long as I could keep Jupiter out of my mind I was fine.

"Frank threw my phone in the bushes, but he didn't count on me having this." From out of my pocket I pulled my Bluetooth and hooked it around my ear. With one press of the small button at its center, it would dial out from my cell phone. As long as my phone was closer than thirty feet away, we were golden.

"You going to call the cops?" she demanded.

"I can call anyone I want," I said.

"Show me," she said.

"Who's the third person?" I pressed.

"Some guy named McCarthy," she said. "A friend of Frank's. They've been moving diamond stud earrings for a while now, just small stuff, nothing like this. Mc-Carthy was the original owner of those homing pigeons out there. Frank feeds the diamonds to Oreo, and he flies to McCarthy, then Oreo regurgitates them back up, and McCarthy sells them."

"Oreo?"

"One of the pigeons. He's better trained than the others or regurgitates on demand, or something."

"They feed the diamonds to pigeons?"

Sylvia sighed, as if I was slow, as if using stupid pigeons to transport precious gems was as common as using UPS. "They always have small stones in their craws, you know, to grind up their food. If you feed them small gems, the birds treat them as regular stones and put them in their craws. It's the perfect hiding place. Then, when the birds get to where they're going, they're made to regurgitate the gems."

"How?"

"I don't know. That's McCarthy's job."

"Where does McCarthy live?"

"Washington or Idaho? Far away from here. I want to say that's why the system is foolproof, but Frank is a fool, he's beyond a fool. He's a loser is what he is."

"When is Frank sending Oreo out?"

"Friday, the last I heard. What day is it, Tuesday?"

I nodded, trying to add things up as quickly as I could. Frank overheard Mr. de Guzman telling his business partner about bringing the diamond into the country in Chelsea's ring. He'd wanted to mug Chelsea, but Sylvia convinced him that it would be simpler and cleaner to see if she might simply buy the ring from Chelsea as soon as she got off the plane. She knew what Chelsea looked like from Frank's description, and followed her when she got off the plane and into the crowded ladies' room, where she heard Chelsea ask her mom about stopping at Coffee People for a cappuccino, just as Chelsea and I had guessed. Now, in three days' time, Frank was going to feed the red diamond to a pigeon named Oreo, who was going to fly with it to another state where another guy, McCarthy, would take the gem from the bird's craw and sell it. Then they would all split the money.

I'd started to sweat. I thought about taking my hoodie off, but if we heard Frank return, I'd want to jump back on my chair and pretend my hands were still tied. Putting my sweatshirt back on would take too much time.

"So, you going to call the cops now and get us the hell out of here?"

"In a minute," I said. There were a few huge holes in the story. Like where was the diamond now, and why had Frank locked Sylvia in the shed?

Sylvia stood up. She was one of those people who seemed taller than she was. "How old are you anyway?" she asked.

"You said Frank stuck you in here because you wouldn't bend to his will."

Every time I mentioned Frank's name Sylvia exploded. I never really knew what it meant when people talked about pressing someone else's button, but I saw how the subject of Frank was Sylvia's button.

"We were going to split three ways, right? Frank, McCarthy, and me. Then the day I get the ring I come here and find Frank in the break room, talking on his cell with McCarthy about how maybe they can cut me out once they get the diamond. I hear Frank say he'll give me a little something for my effort, maybe a grand or two, that that's a lot of money for someone like me.

"I say to him, 'What's to prevent me from just selling the diamond myself?' Frank turns around. He sees me standing there and goes nuts. He can't stand that I've heard his nasty little scheme, and that I still have the diamond and didn't bring it with me. So he throws me in here. He starts telling me that all this is my fault." She stopped and inhaled, collected her thick hair into a ponytail and tied it in a knot at the back of her neck.

"You can do that, too," I said. "Tie your hair in a knot."

"It's hot in here," she said. Her rant about Frank left her exhausted. She wiped the sweat from the bridge of her nose with her sleeve.

I felt sorry for Sylvia, but at the same time didn't trust her. I didn't know how to say what I needed to say in a way that would convince her of my plan. This was a weak point for me, saying things in a convincing way. The only thing I knew how to do was throw the topic out there and start arguing when the other person disagreed. "Sylvia," I said, "if you want to get back at Frank for what he's done to you, you're going to have to give the diamond to him."

She snorted. "There's a fantastic idea."

"Think about it. If I call the police now, they'll come and rescue us, they'll charge Frank with kidnapping, but you won't be able to tell them about Frank and Mc-Carthy without implicating yourself. You're the one who's got the diamond, after all. Frank will say he knows nothing about it. He'll go to jail for kidnapping, but you'll go to jail for having stolen goods."

I wasn't too sure about this—someone could argue that she bought the ring from Chelsea fair and square—but at least I had Sylvia's attention now.

"How do you know?" she asked.

"My dad's a lawyer. And anyway, don't you want to stick it to Frank but good?"

I told her my plan. It felt like skateboarding down a new street I'd never before laid eyes on. I made it up as I went along. The plan had two parts. First, I told her, I would phone Chelsea, who would go to Sylvia's apartment, collect the diamond, and bring it to us. Sylvia would hide it somewhere, as if she'd always had it on her . . .

"Wait a minute," Sylvia interrupted, "you're calling that rich daughter of de Guzman? No way. She'll probably just take the diamond back to her daddy and then when Frank finds out, he'll beat me but good. We call my brother. He knows where the diamond is hidden and how to get here."

"Isn't he on the movie set?"

"If I called him, he would come."

She was probably right. If Sylvia was all he had in the world, he'd be more likely to do what she asked ASAP, even if that meant walking off the set. If I called Chelsea, and she was getting a manicure or riding her horse or whatever, we'd have to wait. And we couldn't afford to wait. I had to take the chance.

I reached beneath my hair, felt for the button on my earpiece. Sure enough, my cell phone was close enough to pick up the signal. I voice dialed the number Sylvia gave me and handed the earpiece to her.

She fumbled as she hooked it around her ear, but caught on to how it worked quick enough.

"Tonio? It's me!" She started to cry again, water-works city. In all my life I've never cried as hard as Sylvia did that moment. We needed to get out of here, and fast.

She spoke to him for a few minutes in Spanish.

Then she hung up and handed me the earpiece. I wondered why she looked so smug. "He's coming immediately. Now it's your turn."

A bad feeling swept over me. Something had shifted. Now Sylvia seemed like the adult that she was and I was the stupid kid. I was in eighth grade. I still had a bed time. I had been in control, and now Sylvia was in control. On the Scale of Scared, I'd inched up to an eight. What I was about to do next was not going to turn out well—the second part of my doomed plan—calling the police.

The not-very-well-thought-out idea was that they would arrive just after Tonio had showed up at the shelter and turned over the diamond to Frank. Then Frank would be in possession of the diamond, and Sylvia and I would still be locked in the shed, kidnapped, held hostage against our will, our lives endangered, and a bunch of other charges that would put Frank in jail for a long time.

I called 911.

My heart lifted a little when I didn't recognize the voice of the operator who answered. It was not the lady with the deep musical blues singer voice, but some woman, probably Sylvia's age, who sounded as if she was from Texas or somewhere.

"I'm being held captive at the animal shelter," I said.

"What is the address," said the operator.

"The address? I don't know. Isn't there only one animal shelter in Portland?" Panic danced in my stomach. "Look, a guy who volunteers here locked me in a shed with another girl. My name is Minerva Clark and—"

"—one moment please," said the operator, cutting me off in mid-sentence.

Then I knew I was doomed. Another person came on the line, my old familiar operator with the old-timey blues singer voice. "Minerva Clark, you've got to stop this. Now

I'm serious, honey. I think you should get yourself some psychological help."

Sylvia didn't seem to mind that the police were not coming. She sat with her legs crossed, tried to clean the grit from beneath her nails, straightened her skirt, arranged her hair a little more. I could tell she was a girl waiting to be rescued.

I tried to keep my mind from straying to thoughts of Jupiter. Just the thought of Frank doing anything to hurt him made tears spring to my eyes. I could not afford to cry, not now. I focused on what everyone said, that Frank loved animals. Even though he was a hateful thief/kidnapper/liar, with a stupid nickname, he was still an animal lover. I tried to picture Jupiter sacked out in one of the nice small animal habitats inside the shelter, safe and sound.

As Sylvia had predicted, Tonio dropped everything. I bet it took him less than half an hour. Outside the shed there was the sound of two people clomping through the urban wilderness, and two voices, Frank's and Tonio's. They sounded all buddy buddy. We heard the screech of the rusty bolt, then the creaky door swung open. The inside of the shed was suddenly bright with sunlight.

I'm not a total dork when it comes to love. I've had an almost-boyfriend, witnessed Reggie mooning over Amanda the Panda, and have seen my parents kiss and make up a thousand times, until they couldn't do it anymore. I thought I was getting a handle on the mystery of love and attraction, but then I saw Sylvia with Frank and realized I didn't know a thing. Here was this creep who'd betrayed her and she still loved him.

I watched, horrified, as she stepped out of the shed and into Frank's arms.

"You're a pain, you know that?" His voice was soft. He ran his hands down her hair.

"You love it," she said. *"Eres tan estupido como un perro."*

I have had one year of Spanish. I think she said, "You are as stupid as a dog."

I should have run. Behind Frank's shoulder I could see the highway, the cars cruising by, but I just stood there. The emergency exit door was propped open as usual, but I just stood there. I glimpsed my phone not far away, shining among the weeds and broken glass, but I just stood there.

I am only in middle school, after all.

Tonio reached into his pocket and produced a piece of duct tape, folded over on itself to make a small packet. Frank plucked it from Tonio's palm, ripped it open, and gazed at the red diamond. It wasn't big, less than a carat, I guessed. It didn't look very impressive, stuck to the silvery tape, just a small piece of something very old and close to perfect that came from deep in the earth.

"I'd say it's time to give Oreo his afternoon snack," said Frank, closing his hand around the diamond. "And tell him he's flying the coop earlier than planned."

For a second I thought they were all just going to walk away and leave me there, which never happened on TV.

Then, faster than a lizard startled while sunning himself, Frank leaped to my side, grabbed me around the neck, and pressed a towel to my face. He moved so fast he even startled cooler-than-thou Tonio, who stood next to his sister, just watching. Frank kept mashing the towel against my face. I tried to wrench myself away, but he was too strong. The towel smelled like Downey, and like the medicine you put on sore muscles. And then I went limp.

– 11 –

I woke up.

Where was I? In another shed? This time there were lights. Bars of neon lights across the low ceiling. Cool cement floor. No windows. Not a shed. Air-conditioning. A small room. Okay, I thought, okay.

Don't freak out. Do not freak out. Hearing your own self scream is one good way to launch a freak-out, so don't do that.

I was lying on my side. It was not the side I normally slept on. I'd been dumped on that side, facing the wall. Concrete wall. My hands weren't tied. Not a good sign. Meant there was nothing easy to do to get myself out of here. Laid there for a minute, listening.

No voices, no traffic. Quiet, except for a low humming sound, a click, a clank.

As soon as I sat up, my head throbbed as if my heart had relocated itself in my skull. It ached as if a steel cap was being slowly tightened by the hand of an unseen torturer. It was a headache out of some horrible sci-fi universe. I didn't know the meaning of headache until that moment.

In a way, this helped me. It hurt so much I couldn't think about how long I'd been there, or whether my brothers were frantic with worry, or whether the brilliant pigeon Oreo had already taken off to find McCarthy and deliver the diamond.

I was thirsty.

I didn't have to pee, so I reasoned that I hadn't been there long. Maybe I'd just gotten there. Maybe it was still broad daylight outside.

I stood up, looked around. Frank had stuck me in a large closet, half the size of my bedroom. It was given over mostly to electrical stuff.

I went to the door and tried the handle. Duh. Of course it was locked. I banged on it for a while with my fists.

"Help!" I yelled. "Help me!"

Hearing myself scream for help made me even more afraid than I already was. No one was coming. No one was going to rescue me.

I looked around the room. On the opposite wall there were things we hadn't even gotten to in basic electronics—I wish I'd paid more attention to bitter old Mr. Lawndale than to Bryce Duncan—big gray boxes with circuit breakers and glass bulbs and spinning meters. There were other gauges with long bars of red, yellow, and green, with a needle sitting smack in the center of the green. There were thick red and blue wires that disappeared into blocks, other wires that were clamped to the wall with oversized screws. There were signs all over the place. DANGER! HIGH VOLTAGE! DO NOT TOUCH!

I had no idea what I was looking at, or how it could be of any help to me. My stomach grumbled. It'd been hours since that bowl of Frosted Mini-Wheats. I could turn off the power, I guess, but what would that accomplish?

In a corner opposite the wall with all the electrical stuff, I spied a dried-out mop that looked as if it hadn't been used in a year, a push broom and dustpan, a few big plastic buckets full of spare parts, spools of copper wire, and a cardboard box of something that looked sort of familiar. I picked one up. It was blue, the size of a salt shaker, with two prongs sticking out of one end. I leaned over and read the side of the box: 400 µF CAPACITORS.

Capacitors . . . weren't those the exploding things from basic electronics?

It's amazing what hope will do for hunger, thirst, and a headache fierce enough to drive your eyeballs right out of their sockets.

I could do this.

I looked around. I needed something to set the capacitor on. Something near the lock. In class, we'd had those pieces of wood called breadboards. I wondered if there was anything like that here. I spied the cleaning supplies, picked up the dustpan, turned it over in my hands. Would this work?

I wedged the dustpan into the crack between the door and the doorjamb, right above the lock. The handle stuck out, creating a little shelf. I set the capacitor on the side of the handle, right next to the door. I went to the electrical side of the closet, found a pair of wires—one red, one black—that disappeared into a fuse box with a giant on/off lever. I pulled the lever down, to off, half expecting the lights to go off, but nothing happened.

That was good. My palms were slick with sweat. I tried to remember just how Mr. Lawndale did it.

I yanked the wires from their clamps. Any pair of wires would work, right? As long as one was positive and one was negative, right? I kept waiting to get zapped but, I reasoned, I lived through one gigantic electric shock—the shock that changed my life—I could survive another one.

Nothing happened. The room hummed with electricity. Click. Clank. I could taste my bad breath from not having eaten.

I tugged the wires across the narrow room to where

the capacitor sat perched on its dustpan shelf wedged into the door beside the lock. I go to a Catholic school even though we Clarks are not Catholic. I knew some patron saints, however. I sent a prayer up to St. Clare, who ran away to become a nun when she was my age. She was the patron saint of television, and not electricity, but it was the best I could do.

I twisted the red wire around the short leg of the capacitor, the black wire around the long leg.

I dashed across the room to the fuse box. My hands were shaking. I flipped on the lever, and crouched low in the corner behind the cleaning supplies.

I waited.

What was taking so long? Maybe I'd done it wrong? Just as I was trying to figure out my next move, the capacitor exploded.

I was deaf, my nose filled with the burnt aroma of melting plastic and that bizarre peanut butter smell. My eyes watered from the smoke. I leaped up, and sure enough, there was a hole the size of my fist by the doorknob. I turned it and the door sprung open and out I went, running down the long dingy hallway, headache gone, hunger gone, thirsty yes, but who cared about thirst? That psycho Frank had stuck me in the basement of some warehouse. At the end of the hallway, up two flights of metal stairs there was a door to outside. I took the stairs two at a time. I could see a thready frame of sunlight around the edges, and I crashed out the door and onto the street, startling a girl in a halter top walking by with her dog on a leash, one of those cute mutts that live forever.

Where was I? I'd been worried that I would make my escape only to find that I was somewhere so foreign that getting home would be as hard as getting out of that stupid closet. But no. The Burnside Bridge loomed up beside me. Straight ahead was Waterfront Park, and then the river. I was on Burnside, the busy main street that separates the north side of Portland from the south side of Portland. I craned my neck, and there, soaring above me atop the roof of the warehouse I'd just busted out of, was the MADE IN OREGON sign, our city's famous landmark.

I knew right where I was. And what I had to do.

There's something called adrenaline, which is a magical drug that your body produces all on its own. It's the fight or flight drug. It makes time slow and pain disappear and helps contribute to that feeling that you might just be an undiscovered superhero. I am going into eighth grade with no special skills and I just almost blew a door off its hinges. When I was a little girl, and used to watch *Star Wars* over and over again with Morgan, I dreamed of being a princess with a blaster. Now I am practically her.

I should have gone straight home to Casa Clark, told Mark Clark I'd been held captive first in a shed, then in an electrical closet, by the same dumb but scary security guard turned jewel thief, asked him to make me one of his special chicken salad sandwiches, let him call the police and file the report and wait for the detectives to come and take my statement, called Chelsea de Guzman and let her know what I'd gone through, all in the name of finding the rare red diamond that had gotten her in trouble with her dad.

I should have, but I was a princess with a blaster, and a mission.

On my way to the bus stop I found a pay phone and called Reggie. Even though I had a cell phone, Mark Clark had drilled into my head the importance of always carrying a couple quarters in your pocket, just in case something happened. I don't think he ever imagined the "something" would be a lunatic throwing my phone into the shrubbery before locking me in a shed.

I dialed Reggie. I had no hope that he would be able to help me, but he answered on the second ring.

"Dude, you are so not going to believe this—"

"Hi, Minerva." Again, his voice was low and flat. He sounded sick.

"Are you all right?"

"Yeah." He was so *not* all right. "What's up?"

"I need an IP. Meet me at the transit center."

"Sure. When?"

I was stunned. "You don't have to hang around in case Amanda the Panda calls or anything?"

"Nah," he said. He sounded as if he was going to cry. I don't think I'd seen Reggie cry since preschool, when one of the kids at the indoor play gym bashed him in the head with a toy dump truck.

Why more kids my age don't take advantage of our city's great public transportation system, I don't know. It beats riding your bike, travels just about anywhere you'd need to go. I hopped on the MAX. I was a little delirious that Reggie was going to meet me. I hadn't seen him in what felt like forever.

I didn't know what time it was. It was still glary bright outside, but it could have been dinnertime. Summer in the northwest is deceiving. It doesn't get dark until nine o'clock. Five o'clock p.m. feels like noon. My white hoodie with the blue Hawaiian flowers marching up the sleeve was filthy. I tied it around my waist.

When I got off at the transit center, Reggie was already there. His mom must have dropped him off. He stood under a tree with his hands shoved deep in his back pockets, making his saggy pants sag even more. Why boys thought this was a worthwhile style of dress, I'll never know. His thick bangs hung in his eyes, which were such a dark green they almost looked black. He smiled when he saw me, but it wasn't his normal big goofy Reggie smile. He looked tired.

I was pretty much out of my mind with joy to see him, but couldn't tell Reggie that.

On the number 10 bus, I filled him in on everything, chattering like Chelsea de Guzman after she'd had too many lattes. Usually, Reggie is not very good at listening. He interrupts when he gets a big idea. He can't help it. The only thing he asked was where we were going.

"To the humane society. You gotta take a look at this pigeon coop thing. That's where Frank is hiding the diamond. Or actually, he's hiding it in the craw of that bird Oreo. That's kind of a great idea, isn't it? Who would ever look inside a bird?"

"Pretty excellent," said Reggie.

"He was supposed to send Oreo out Friday to McCarthy, the guy who's fencing the jewel, but since I found out about it he's sending Oreo out earlier. How can we intercept him, do you think?"

"You mean, how do you intercept a homing pigeon on its route?" he asked.

"Yeah, something like that."

I glanced over at Reggie, slumped in the seat beside me. Normally, this was just the sort of thing Reggie was into. Ask him the smallest question about how lions hunt, or mention that bats can see in the dark, and he becomes a walking, talking one-man science exhibit.

I thought homing pigeons, with their ability to fly hundreds of miles and never get lost, would be something Reggie could geek out on for hours. He would know about strapping a tiny radio transmitter to the pigeon's back and building a receiver, or implanting it with some radioactive I don't know what that we could trace using something else I'd never heard of.

But Reggie just sat. "I don't know," he said.

This was too much.

I stared out the window. We passed a bakery thrift shop. I made a joke about who would want someone else's old bagels and muffins. Reggie just stared at the back of the seat in front of him.

"*What* is wrong with you?" I asked.

He kept staring at the seatback. "Amanda broke up with me," he mumbled, and then I think he started to cry.

This was not good. I was a princess with a blaster in the middle of solving a mystery. I needed him to help me intercept Oreo. I didn't know what to do. I didn't dare look over. Reggie, on the bus, crying. It was impossible. I thought about what my brothers would do, but I wasn't one of my brothers. "I'm sorry," I managed. That's what people said to me when my grandpa died, and Reggie seemed that wrecked. This wasn't like when you're crushing on someone for a week or two, then sort of forget about them when there's a long weekend and you don't see them for four days. This was genuine heartbreak.

Crap.

He got himself together then, blotted his eyes with his hands, cleared his throat. "It's like that," he pointed at the front of my Green Day T-shirt.

I looked down, and read upside down: **I ♥ GD**.

The heart is a hand grenade.

The parking lot at the humane society was almost empty. A few cars sat parked at the far end. The shelter was closed. The pretty new building cast a long shadow on the vacant lot behind it. I knew Frank worked all his jobs part time, so I crossed my fingers he'd already left for his security guard job. I doubt he'd show up at the de Guzmans' to walk the dogs. Just to make double sure he was gone, Reggie and I knelt behind an old car and watched the pigeon coop for ten or fifteen minutes. There was nothing. No one came in or out. The place was deserted.

"This is kind of cool out here," said Reg. I could tell he was trying to get in the spirit of things, but I realized that I wasn't going to be able to count on him much; still, it was good to have the company.

"What should we do?"

"Well, you blew the door off that closet. We could always blow up the pigeon coop."

"Ha ha," I said.

"I don't know. I think the best idea is just to steal the bird."

"Thank you, drive through please," I said.

"Can you think of anything else?" he said.

"No, I can't. That's why you're here, Mr. Brainiac."

"Steal the bird, that's my idea."

"How do we know which one is Oreo?"

"Probably, he looks like an Oreo. Or the bird version of an Oreo."

"Great," I said.

Even though I was hands down the Most Awesome Escape Artist in my entire family and was full of magical adrenaline, I was still dead afraid of birds.

We crunched through the brush, past the Dumpsters in their tidy little storage pen, through the gap in the chain-link fence, to the pigeon coop. I could hear the evil birds cooing from inside. The human entrance for the coop was on one end of the water tank. It was one of those black wrought iron security doors some people have in place of a screen door. I didn't want Reggie to think I was some stupid girly girl afraid of birds, so I didn't stop and think.

To stop and think would be to stop and run away screaming. I pretended birds didn't bother me in the least. No worries, I thought. Pretend they're ferrets, ferrets with feathers and wings. The door wasn't locked or anything. I walked right in, with Reg right behind me.

I want to say there were eight thousand pigeons, all of whom fixed me with their evil Jell-O bird eyes and prepared to peck my guts out, but only a few dozen birds were ambling here and there on their red feet, paying me no mind at all. The window at the opposite end of the tank was affixed with perches, and the floor was made of wooden slats, probably so Frank or someone could clean out the massive amount of bird poop.

The birds were mostly white, smaller than I expected. They had slim necks, some with iridescent feathers. A few had gray stripes on their wings.

"Check it out," whispered Reggie. "There's your bird."

He pointed to a bird sitting on one of the window perches. He was all black with white wings and a white band around his middle, just like an Oreo.

Perhaps it was the heat, or maybe these birds were used to humans, but as I reached out to grab Oreo, he didn't screech or flutter his wings, or try to bite me. He wasn't like Jupiter, he didn't back away, fluff his wings, quake with fear. He looked bored and turned his back, which allowed me to drop my hoodie on top of him, scoop him up, dash out of the coop, and trot through the field toward the street. We jogged a block or two until I spied Patsy's, the hamburger joint. There was a service station with a pay phone on the corner. I fished for a quarter in my back pocket and called home.

- 12 -

It was nearly nine o'clock when I walked through the door of Casa Clark with a pigeon wrapped in my sweatshirt, hours late for dinner. I spied the time on the big kitchen clock over the sink, where Mark Clark was washing the dinner dishes, in his business-casual khakis and pink polo shirt.

It must have been just him and Quills at the big dining room table that night. Morgan was still camping out somewhere in the desert of Eastern Oregon. It looked as if Mark Clark had made my favorite spaghetti dish, angel hair with Parmesan and black olives. I knew I was in deep trouble because he wasn't listening to his eighties music on his boom box, something he normally does when he's in the kitchen. He scrubbed the pots with too much energy and his mouth was a thin line inside the circle of his goatee. I was too exhausted to worry about the trouble I was in.

I'd spent the short ride from the service station to Casa Clark trying to explain my day to Quills, who kept looking over at me from beneath raised eyebrows. I sat between Quills and Reggie, who looked out the window a lot and sighed. Nabbing Oreo had distracted him for a while, but now he was back to moping. Poor Reggie.

Oreo sat on my lap, swaddled in my hoodie. He was very still. I worried that maybe I'd suffocated him—you would think I wouldn't mind, given my hatred of birds—but I was grateful to him for having allowed me to pick him up without trying to peck my eyes out. I didn't want anything bad to happen to him, at least while he was being kidnapped by me.

"So let me get this straight," said Quills. I could hear the smile in his voice. "First, you busted out of an abandoned shed at the humane society . . ."

"Behind the humane society in a vacant lot. And I didn't bust out. Frank let us out, because Tonio, Sylvia's brother, brought Frank the diamond. Then the cops were supposed to arrive and catch Frank red-handed, with hostages *and* the stolen diamond, but they didn't show up . . ."

"You called the cops and they didn't show up?" asked Quills.

"It's a long story . . ." I said. "But I thought Sylvia was

on my side. When we were being held captive, she acted like she hated Frank. Then Tonio showed up and Frank let her out and suddenly they were all lovey-dovey."

"And that's when Frank chloroformed you . . ."

"He put a towel against my face with something that smelled like medicine and that made me sleepy."

"Sounds like chloroform to me. Straight out of some bad seventies detective show."

"I don't know." I peeked inside the small bundle on my lap, even reached in and touched Oreo's black feathers with my finger.

"Here's a question for ya," continued Quills. "Why would Louis de Guzman hide an expensive gem in his thirteen-year-old's ring instead of shipping it? The guy's loaded. He needed to save the hundred bucks or something?"

"Big-time jewelers do it all the time, Quills! Don't they, Reggie? Don't say it like it's this unbelievably ridiculous thing! And if I'm lying, then what were Reg and I doing out on Columbia Boulevard? I didn't have anything better to do than steal a pigeon out of a pigeon coop? 'Cause you know how much I love birds."

"Well, it's not just any pigeon! It's got de Guzman's red diamond hidden in its craw. Mwa-ha-ha!" He laughed his phony evil bad guy laugh.

The air-conditioning was on high in the Electric Matador—Quills's old Ford Ranchero with the bullhorns strapped to the front—but it didn't work, just blew warm air into my neck. I really wished Quills would get off my back. He could be a real pain sometimes. We drove for a few blocks, passed El Taco Loco, where they have the best three-dollar burritos on earth.

"You hungry?" asked Quills. His voice had softened. He was trying to make amends, but that just irritated me more. It was that boy way of saying you're sorry, where you just act nice all of a sudden.

"I feel as if I'm about to hurl, actually," I said.

We rode in silence. I didn't even reach over to turn on the radio.

"You gotta admit, Min, this all sounds pretty far-fetched." Quills tried again.

"Look, before last week I hadn't even heard of red diamonds. I didn't even know they existed. I was just looking for something to do—you and Mark Clark are on me all the time about finding something to do, so I found something to do! You don't understand. I had that stupid accident and it made me so different from every girl I know. Before I thought I was ugly and awful, but at least that's something girls my age understand. I don't want to go to the mall and try on lip gloss. I don't want to obsess about my clothes. It would be a whole lot easier if I did, believe me!"

Quills didn't say another word.

Then Reggie did a strange thing: He reached over and

patted my hand, then held it there. It felt all right, having Reggie hold my hand, although I did something that was probably not very nice: I closed my eyes and pretended he was Kevin. Then Quills dropped Reggie off at his house, and my brother and I drove home in silence.

Mark Clark sat at the dining room table with his arms crossed and listened to the whole mad story. Oreo sat on the floor of Jupiter's wire cage in the middle of the dining room table. We couldn't think of anything else to do with him. He stood in the middle of the cage and looked around.

The more I told the story, the more impossible it seemed, even to me. At home I no longer felt like a princess with a blaster. My shoulders hurt. My back hurt. The inside of my *ears* hurt. How is that even possible? From the explosion maybe?

Mark Clark chuckled when I got to the part about using the capacitor to blow off the lock on the electrical closet door. He couldn't resist saying that he knew I'd like basic electronics.

"Quills thinks I'm lying," I blurted out. I couldn't help saying that. It was the sight of that stupid bird in Jupiter's cage. Where was Jupiter? Was he gone forever? I slumped into a chair at the table, put my head on my arms, and cried like an idiot. "They took Jupiter, too." I cried even harder.

My brothers just sat there. They are boys, and this is what boys do when you cry. They sit there and wait for it to be over.

"Well, I don't think you're lying," said Mark Clark. "But I do think you're engaging in what they now call high-risk activity, but used to be called being just plain stupid."

"How was I being stupid? I went to the humane society to talk to somebody. It was in public. I didn't get in his car or anything. It wasn't my fault that the guy I thought was Shark turned out to be Frank, the de Guzmans' dog sitter. It's not my fault Chelsea turned up and told him everything, is it?"

Mark Clark rubbed his forehead. I could sense he thought I had a point.

"Anyway," I went on, "you can blame Morgan. I was about to just quit looking for the diamond, but he said that sometimes you just have to pursue something because it's there and because it interests you."

Mark Clark said nothing. We watched Oreo peck around the bottom of the cage. Finally, Mark Clark said, "So there's a red diamond sitting in the craw of this bird."

"Well, I think so. I knew they were sending a bird named Oreo out with the diamond, and this was the only bird in the coop that looked like an Oreo."

"I can see that," said Mark Clark.

"It's actually kind of a cool plan," I said. "Use the bird to hide the gem and transport it at the same time."

"And who were they sending it to, again?"

"Some guy named McCarthy, who lives pretty far away, in Washington or Idaho or somewhere. He was the one who was going to sell the diamond and split the money."

"He must be the fence," says Quills. "You're getting into some pretty sophisticated crime stopping if you're dealing with a fence." He sat on the edge of the table, poking a chopstick between the bars of the cage.

"Stop mocking me!" I shouted. I couldn't take it another minute.

"I think we should just call the police," said Mark Clark.

"I think we should make ol' Oreo here toss his cookies, see what we got," said Quills.

"Good idea," I said quickly.

"Throw up?" said Mark Clark.

"Regurgitate. Whatever."

They both considered Oreo with new interest.

"I don't know that it's so easy," said Mark Clark. "I read something once about a macaw that ate one of its owner's diamond earrings. They couldn't get the bird to regurgitate the earring no matter what they did. By the time surgery was done to recover the earring, the facets on the diamond had all been blunted. That's how long the earring was in there."

"Let's give him a little dish of mustard and water and see what happens."

Quills disappeared into the kitchen and returned with a jar lid half full of a runny yellow substance. He slid it inside Jupiter's cage. The bird wouldn't go near it. We decided perhaps we needed to try the Internet, and trooped into the computer room to peer over Mark Clark's shoulder as he Googled "how to make a bird throw up."

All the first aid for birds Web sites said that you should never try to make a bird throw up, in capital letters. They didn't say why.

"But the diamond is in his craw, not his stomach, right?" said Mark Clark.

"Aren't they the same thing?" I asked.

"I think the craw is the pre-stomach," said Quills. "The storage area for the stomach."

It was dark now. The only light in the room shone from the computer monitor. Outside, crickets chirped. We all got along much better this way, trying to solve a problem that didn't have much to do with any of us. I wonder what my life would have been like if we'd had a sister. Then I thought, Morgan was like the sister, but he was out communing with nature.

Then, on one site we found something: What to do if your bird has "craw-emptying problems."

"Give it a few drops of Maalox and massage craw gently."

"What's Maalox?" I said.

"Medicine for an upset stomach," said Quills.

As I was leaning on Mark Clark's shoulder, peering at the screen, I felt my eyes ease shut. I felt like Dorothy in *The Wizard of Oz,* stumbling around the poppy field. So tired, all of a sudden. I sat down on the futon on the other side of the computer. Unlike my bedroom on the third floor, which would be hot and stuffy, the computer room was on the east side of the house, and had windows that would allow a nice breeze.

I closed my eyes, listened while Mark Clark and Quills talked about whether we had any of this Maalox in the house, or whether Pepto-Bismol would do. It seemed they'd forgotten how the bird got here, and were now involved completely in how to get it to cough up the diamond. That was good. I felt the weight of all my mystery solving drift off me.

I heard Mark Clark and Quills leave the room . . . kitchen cupboards opening and closing . . . laughter . . . fridge opening and closing . . . talking . . . Jupiter's cage door opening and closing . . . Quills saying "You hold him" . . . Mark Clark saying "There we go, there we go . . ."

Then, suddenly, something made me open my eyes, a strange feeling that I wasn't alone.

Before me in the blue light of the computer screen stood Frank. He was wearing his security guard uniform. Around his waist he wore a thick leather belt, with one of those big black sticks hanging off one side. I felt my throat close. He also had a gun, big and black, stuck in a holster on his hip.

I shot up from the futon, wide awake. "Mark!" I yelled.

"What are you doing here?" I said loudly. I shouted Mark's name again.

"I really didn't think you'd be this much trouble, Suzanne," sighed Frank. "You seemed like a really nice girl."

"How did you find my house?" I croaked.

"You put it down on the application at the humane society," he said, glancing around the room. "I just want my bird."

"Yeah, well, I want my ferret. Where's my ferret?"

Mark Clark appeared at the doorway, then Quills behind him. The room was bathed in computer screen light. We Clarks are not small people. My brothers are both six feet. But so was Frank.

Mark Clark said, "What the . . ." and Quills yelled, "What's going on here?" Suddenly, there seemed to be a lot of us in that small, dark room.

With his tufts of crayon yellow hair and black T-shirt that says IT'S NOT REVENGE, IT'S PUNISHMENT, and weight-lifter's biceps, Quills looks like the bigger threat. Frank stepped toward him. He put his hand on his belt.

What Frank couldn't know, of course, is that Mark

Clark, the dictionary definition of computer geek, spent most of seventh grade suspended from school. In sixth grade he was a chubby boy with braces and glasses who got beat up every day at the bus stop. Then over the summer, Mark Clark grew three inches. The braces came off and he switched his Coke bottle glasses for contact lenses. He didn't fully come into his self-confidence until first period, on the first day of seventh grade, when one of his old nemeses started in and Mark Clark hauled him over his desk by his collar and popped him in the nose. He then spent most of seventh grade beating up everyone who'd ever made fun of him.

I'm saying all this because the point is, most people think they know how to take someone down. They've seen it in the movies, but they've never done it themselves. It's not about breaking chairs over each other's heads and turning the other guy into a punching bag. If done right, it never lasts long.

Mark Clark strode past Quills, grabbed Frank by the collar, pulled his arm back, and smashed him smack in the middle of his forehead with his fist. Frank fell into a heap.

Quills swore and leaped back into the hallway. Mark Clark shouted, "Get the hell out of my house!" but Frank had managed to roll onto his side and slide his gun from its holster. He pointed it straight at Mark Clark.

"Come on, man!" said Quills, throwing his hands in the air.

"You have your little sister to thank for this," said Frank.

"Minerva, go call the police," said Mark Clark.

But I had an even better idea.

"Hey! Get back here!" I heard Frank call out after me as I stalked out of the computer room. I was holding my breath. I ran down the hallway and into the dining room, where I unlatched Jupiter's cage, picked up Oreo gently by his sides. He still fixed me with his Jell-O eye, but I wasn't afraid of him at all. "Come on, Oreo, be a good boy. Do what you do.

"I've got your stupid bird!" I called out.

Back down the hallway I went, the bird held out in front of me. I stopped in front of the computer room. "You want your bird? Here's your bird."

Quills stood in the hallway looking alarmed. I could tell he couldn't figure out what I was doing. Mark Clark turned away from Frank, and in that moment Frank struggled to his feet, blood running down his face. I couldn't tell whether his nose was broken, or what.

Before anyone could move a muscle, I pushed open the back door. The screen door wasn't latched. I bumped it open with my hip, whispered to Oreo, "Fly home, boy," and tossed him in the air.

Oreo circled the driveway once, then disappeared into

the still summer night. I didn't know whether he would go back to the pigeon coop at the animal shelter, or on to McCarthy's coop, hundreds of mile away. I don't know much about birds. But my scheme worked: Releasing Oreo got rid of Frank, who pushed past my brothers and staggered out of the house and down the driveway. We watched as his white pickup truck roared off.

Mark Clark called 911, and because he's not a thirteen-year-old pest itchy to solve a mystery, they sent a squad car right over. The officers were both as wide as they were tall, with buzz cuts and sunburns; that's what a few days of northwest sun will do to you at the beginning of summer.

They were concerned mostly with the trespassing portion of the story, and with Frank threatening us with a weapon, and when exactly Mark Clark punched Frank, and whether his weapon had already been pulled, and so on.

When we backed into the part of the story that featured the black-and-white homing pigeon called Oreo, which I'd taken from the coop behind the Portland Humane Society, after having blown off the door to the electrical closet in the downtown warehouse on which the MADE IN OREGON sign was perched, after having been held hostage with another female in a shed behind the Portland Humane Society, having come in search of said woman's boyfriend, who only worked at the animal shelter to pick up chicks, according to said woman's younger brother, who was currently costarring in the new Rodney von Lager movie—they'd heard of that; one of their buddies from the force had been assigned to provide security on the set—they'd closed their notebooks and said that they would need to refer all this to the FBI.

Something about moving stolen property over state lines.

After they took off, Mark Clark hugged me close to him and said, "You did not have to do that, you know."

"Do what?"

"Save my neck by sending that nutcase out after the bird."

"Well, clearly I *did*," I said. "You having a gun pointed at your head and all."

Then we didn't say anything else. Quills made popcorn, with lots of butter and salt, and we all sat together in a row and watched *Charlie and the Chocolate Factory* for about the tenth time.

Between cracking jokes about the Oompa Loompas, all of whom were played by the same strange guy, we pieced together what happened: Frank probably checked out the pigeon coop, and when he saw that Oreo was gone, he'd headed straight to the warehouse where he'd held me captive. We figured he knew about the closet because he worked at the building as their security guard.

When he'd seen that I'd managed to escape, he came here.

We wondered if the diamond would ever make it to McCarthy, and how do you get a bird to regurgitate a diamond anyway? We wondered how many millions the diamond was actually worth. Then the brothers started talking about what they'd do with that much money, and the subject of Harley-Davidson motorcycles came up, and then I fell asleep sitting up, something I almost never do.

– 13 –

The next morning Mark Clark let me sleep in. The sun was high in the sky when I showed up downstairs, the breakfast dishes still on the table. They'd had Mark Clark's German pancakes. I could tell from the syrup lakes left on the plates. At my place, a yellow pancake sat untouched, browned just a little at the edges, all the bubbles deflated into buttery folds. Yum. I was starving. The dining room windows were open. Outside, I could hear someone mowing his lawn.

It seemed like a Saturday, because Mark Clark had taken the day off work. The FBI was supposed to call, to open an investigation about Frank and McCarthy's jewel thieving operation. I didn't really have much hope the FBI would get them. One of the things I'd learned when I solved my last mystery is that you can pretty much accuse anyone of anything, but unless there are enough witnesses to make up a marching band, obvious motive, and boatloads of what they call forensic evidence—fingerprints, hair and fiber samples, stuff like that—they're bound to walk. The courts are too crowded with cases, and the jails are too crowded with prisoners. In our city, the rumor is, if you steal a car, you get a parking ticket. That's how it is.

I ate my pancake, saving the soft middle part for last, and read the comics. I was disappointed. I'd solved the mystery, but hadn't caught the bad guys. If you don't catch the bad guys, what's the point? I thought about Sherlock Holmes and Nancy Drew and then about all the real-life private detectives out there: You never hear about the cases that are left open.

I took my plate into the kitchen. Mark Clark came in and tousled my hair.

"We've got to find Jupiter," I said.

"I made a call to the humane society this morning," said Mark Clark, "wondering if they had an extra ferret lying around. They said they had a nice fat white one that had just come in."

"Jupiter's not fat!" I said, smiling. "Can we go get him now?"

"Get dressed," he said.

I have one skirt for summer, with tiers of crinkled white cotton. I put it on with a yellow T-shirt and my new turquoise Chuck Taylors. I always got in trouble for not wearing socks, but I was pretty sure I'd be able to get away with it today.

I stepped in front of the mirror on the back of my door, inspected myself. While on the bus on the way back to the humane society to steal Oreo, I'd wondered whether perhaps the explosion had blown my strange self-acceptance clean out of me. If an electric shock could alter my sense of self, it made perfect sense that the blast from a mis-wired capacitor could alter it yet again. I studied myself in the mirror for a few long minutes, waiting for some feeling of self-hatred or criticism to surge up inside, but there was nothing. I was still the same old new me, with my snarly mass of hair and long arms. If I ever became famous, this hair could become my trademark. I would never straighten it or dye it, like every other famous girl on the planet. Have you noticed that? The moment they become famous, the first thing they do is change themselves so they look like everybody else.

My legs were as pale as mushrooms. I decided that after we retrieved Jupiter I would sit out in the backyard.

I skipped downstairs, enjoying the way my skirt went all floaty with each step. I was still staring down at my hem when I stepped out of the back door. Between the driveway and the house, there is a narrow bed of dirt where nothing ever grows. Every year my mom would stick some plant in there and water it to death, and fertilize it, but nothing ever took hold.

As I passed the bed, I noticed something small and shiny. I bent to pick it up.

It was a small red gem, a diamond you could have mistaken for a piece of broken glass.

Mr. de Guzman asked us to bring the diamond to the house. As Mark Clark and I drove up, Chelsea opened the front door to greet us. Winkin', Blinkin', and Ned squirted out the door, ran around in delirious doggy circles. Winkin' or Blinkin'—I could never tell them apart—dashed with his tongue hanging out to the center of the lawn and started digging. Ned trotted up and leaned against my shins, waiting for me to reach down and pet him. I ran my hand up and down his thick white fur with its lone ginger patch over his shoulder. I still could not believe that he wasn't good enough to be a show dog. To me, he was the best dog ever.

"Oh my God, this is soooooo amazing!" Chelsea jumped around in her striped halter top and torn jeans, clapping her hands and patting me on the back with both hands. It occurred to me that some people are born to be cheerleaders, and Chelsea de Guzman was one. "Let's see, let's see, let's see."

I'd wrapped the diamond in some Kleenex and stuck it in an empty case of dental floss, just like Mrs. de Guzman said she used to do. Chelsea gasped when she saw it. "It's in *there*? Eeew!"

"What do you mean? It's just dental floss."

"I don't know," she said, then laughed and skipped inside.

Mr. de Guzman didn't seem to think there was anything strange about the dental floss case. He took the case from me and led us all into his study. He had thick gray hair that was cut to curl over his ears in a fashionable way, and white movie star teeth. "You caught me just as I was leaving for my golf game. You golf, Mark?"

"Not if I can help it," said Mark Clark.

"That's how I feel," said Chelsea. "Daddy makes me go anyway."

Mr. de Guzman sat down at his desk and turned on his gooseneck lamp, even though it was broad daylight. I leaned over his shoulder. He smelled like cinnamon and aftershave.

"I am frankly stunned at what a nuisance this diamond has turned out to be. I was just doing this as a favor to Rodney in exchange for credit at the end of his film. You know, sort of a product endorsement thing."

He took out a small round magnifying glass—a jeweler's loupe—and a pair of tweezers and laid them on the blotter, then dumped out the Kleenex-wrapped gem. He carefully unwrapped it, rolled it around on the blotter with his finger. "The lesson to be learned here . . ." he said, as he put the loupe to his eye, and plucked up the diamond with his tweezers.

I thought he was going to say that you should be more careful with such a rare and valuable thing as this.

". . . is that beautiful gems make people do crazy things. We always thought of Frank as one of the family. Who could imagine he'd get up to something like this." He shook his head. Mr. de Guzman was pretty handsome for a dad.

"The FBI is going to investigate," said Mark Clark. "From what Minerva says, Frank and his partner don't seem like rocket scientists."

"I think they'll be surprised to find it's much tougher to move these loose gems then people think," said Mr. de Guzman.

He put the loupe close to his eye, brought the diamond up to the loupe.

"Maybe the diamond is cursed," I said. "Like the Hope diamond."

Mr. de Guzman had an easy laugh. He wasn't as stern as I remembered him to be the day I saw him in his gray suit at parent conferences. "I seriously hope not," he said.

He put down the loupe and the tweezers and turned and looked at me. "You're a pretty unusual girl, aren't you?" he said.

"I don't think so," I said. "I'm probably taller than most girls my age."

"This diamond is a fake, Minerva. I'm sorry you went to so much trouble to find it."

"What do you mean?"

"It's cubic zirconium. Probably worth about thirty bucks."

"I don't understand. I found it in the dirt beside our back door. It came straight out of the craw of the pigeon Frank was using to move the diamond."

"I don't know what to tell you. It's not the diamond I purchased in London."

"Daddy, that's totally impossible," cried Chelsea. "It has to be the diamond. Minerva like practically got killed trying to help me. She's my best friend!" Chelsea slung her arm around my shoulder and hugged me to her. "I like that skirt," she said.

"I just don't know what to tell you," said Mr. de Guzman. "We do appreciate what you've done for us."

I sat down on one of the white couches. I stared at the matchy matchy paintings on the wall. I drew Ned up onto my lap.

"I think I know who's got the real diamond," I said.

"You do?" asked Chelsea, her eyes wide. "Cool."

It *was* cool, because Mr. de Guzman had an expression on his face that said he was all ears, and Mark Clark didn't attempt to silence me by saying, "I think that's enough mystery solving for one day, Minerva!" They looked at me, and they waited.

I thought back to Sylvia's conversation with Tonio, the one conducted all in Spanish. I realized now that she hadn't wanted me to understand. I thought back to the small silver packet Tonio had produced there at the shed, with the diamond stuck to the duct tape. The diamond hadn't looked special, because it wasn't special. Sylvia had instructed her devoted brother to bring another gem, pried from one of her own pieces of jewelry. By the time Frank would have sent Oreo out to McCarthy and McCarthy would have recovered the diamond from Oreo's craw, Sylvia and Tonio would be back in Puerto Vallarta. Frank had tried to double-cross Sylvia, but it was Sylvia who'd wound up double-crossing Frank. Even though Tonio and Sylvia hadn't started out as partners in crime, they'd ended up that way.

The night before, the patrolmen had given Mark Clark a phone number to call if he thought of anything else. He called the police. Mr. de Guzman smiled and said, "You *are* an unusual girl."

After we left the de Guzmans' house Mark Clark and I picked up Jupiter at the humane society. He was in a nice cage in the small animal section, with a tag on his cage that said: "I'm lovable, but I like to stick my nose into other people's business!"

Just for the heck of it Mark Clark marched up to the

front desk and asked whether Frank was working that day. The woman working there said she'd heard he'd up and quit. We went around to the junkyard urban wilderness in the back to see if we could find my phone. There was yellow crime scene tape strung across the gap in the chain-link fence. Mark said to forget the phone, he'd buy me another one. But then I saw something glinting in the sun. I ducked beneath the tape, trotted through the weeds and debris, and snatched it up. I wiped the dust from it with my hand. The battery was dead, but otherwise it looked as if it still worked.

When we got home Morgan was in the backyard, stretching his sleeping bag out on the picnic table.

"Better move that before Mom gets here," said Mark Clark. "She called and said she might be early."

Morgan ignored him. I asked him how the desert was, and he asked me did I find out anything about that diamond. I said I did. He said good.

Sometimes it's just so nice having brothers. Things wouldn't be so simple when mom showed up. I ran into the kitchen to put my phone on its charger. Mark Clark's phone rang. It was the police.

"Some detectives went over to Sylvia Soto's apartment," said Mark after he'd hung up. "She and her brother have apparently cleared out. Their apartment was empty, and the brother didn't show up on Rodney von Lager's movie set today either. They've put out an all-points bulletin for them. And for Frank, too."

"Do you think they'll actually catch them?" I asked.

"If they do, I'm sure they'll let us know," said Mark Clark.

My question about whether the police would ever find Sylvia was answered later that day, when I went to Chelsea's house to hang for a bit. She'd called and asked me to come over. I grabbed my phone and set out.

I passed the mailman on the front walkway. He said "howdy" as he went on his way. Chelsea stood in the doorway with an armful of magazines and catalogues, reading a postcard, her eyebrows crinkled with confusion or worry or something. I'd never seen her look that way.

"And I thought we got a lot of dumb catalogues at our house," I said, nodding at the pile of slick catalogues.

"This is bizarre," she said.

She handed me the card.

As postcards go, it couldn't have been more boring. On the front it said Portland International Airport in fancy writing, and pictured a big silver jet on the runway, with snowy Mt. Hood in the background. I turned it over. It was addressed to "Chelsea and Her Nosy Friend."

"I guess you're the Nosy Friend," said Chelsea.

The card read:

Mi Amigas:

I just wanted to say . . . you are both GEMS! Well, got to catch my plane. Tonio says hello!

Adios!

Sylvia

"What do you think it means?" asked Chelsea, turning and leading me into their all white living room.

I laughed. "That we'll never see them again. Unless we go to Puerto Vallarta."

Chelsea sat on the edge of the white sofa, smoothed her hair against her head. "Well, here's the thing," she said. "My mom has a question for you. My mom is so lame sometimes. She tries to be cool, but sometimes she is just lame."

"What's the question?" I asked.

"You don't have to say yes. I mean, just because we're best friends, don't think you have to do it. I know sometimes—like with Julia last year when she wanted me to go to that dance at her boyfriend's school way out in some horrible suburb—I can't even remember where—you just feel like you have to, but you don't have to. This is a way bigger thing than some stupid dance."

It's a good thing Chelsea was the breed standard of cute, because otherwise she was sure annoying. *"What. Is. It?"*

Then, at that moment, before Chelsea could say

another word, my cell phone made a sound I hadn't heard in the longest time, the semi-embarrassing *tring-tring-triiiiiiinnnng* that tells me I have a message.

"Hold on a sec."

I popped my Bluetooth over my ear. I had three messages.

All from Kevin.

"Minerva, it's me, Kevin. I'm somewhere . . . around Missoula? We just got phone service. I'll call you back."

"Minerva, okay, your phone's still not on. We're in Idaho or something. I really tried to call, but there was no phone service. Oh, man. I hope you're not totally mad at me."

"Min? We just stopped at a 7-Eleven and I got you some of those tropical Starbursts that you like. Well, actually, I got about a dozen packages, so I could pick out all the kiwi banana ones. Those are your favorites, right? Call me!"

Before this moment, I never knew what people meant when they said they were in a swoon. But now I was in one. I felt as if I was going to float up to the ceiling like a birthday balloon. Each new message was better than any Christmas present I'd ever received. I sat down on the sofa.

"Who was *that*?" asked Chelsea. "Your face is all red."

"Remember that guy I took to the last dance?"

"That total hottie you were slow-dancing with?"

Before I could answer, there was the sound of doggie toenails on the wood floor. It was Ned, on his leash, followed by Mrs. de Guzman.

"Well?" she said.

"Mom! I haven't had a chance to ask her yet! She was on the phone with her boyfriend. Jeez. She wants you to take Ned," said Chelsea.

"Ned the dog?"

"Now that we've lost our dog sitter, we can't keep all three of them," said Mrs. de Guzman. "And you and Ned seemed to have really hit it off."

In the Clark house we have a motto: It's always easier to ask forgiveness than it is to ask permission. I hoped the brothers would remember this as I walked home with my new dog, Ned, trotting along beside me on his leash. I'd been held hostage twice this week, and helped break a jewel-thief ring. I'd been traumatized. The least they could do was let me have a dog.

Cloud 9 was way too low a cloud number to describe my mood. It was more like Cloud 999. Kevin would be home Friday! I tried to think of a way to get out of basic electronics, which was coming up.

It was slow going; Ned stopped to mark every tree between Chelsea's house and Casa Clark. This is Portland, Oregon; there are *a lot* of trees.

Mrs. de Guzman had packed Ned's wardrobe of

collars and rain jackets, his chewy toys and bowls, into a burlap tote bag from her tote bag collection. She said she had a million of them. They were always the special presents you got for donating money to public television. The bag wasn't light.

As Ned and I strolled along I couldn't help wondering whether the red diamond would ever be recovered. Maybe it wasn't just a face-in-the-crowd diamond after all, but every bit as cursed as the Hope diamond. Look at the stupid things people had done for it. Including trying to sneak it into the country in a cheap six-dollar ring. Of course, people didn't need a diamond in their lives to do ridiculous things. Love made people just as silly. Look at Reggie and Amanda the Panda, and Frank and Sylvia, and even Kevin, with his dozen packages of tropical Starbursts fruit chews.

I was feeling all wise and happy as I turned up the street that led to Casa Clark. Life could not be better. Then, as I reached our driveway, I spied my mom's old white Pathfinder parked in the driveway. I knew it was her from the New Mexico plates. The car was covered with dust from the drive. She and her boyfriend Rolando were early.

And then I saw it.

It took a minute to register.

On the back of the car windshield were written the words "Just Married."

Acknowledgments

My deep appreciation goes to Chris Fletcher and Mitch Finnegan, two fine veterinarians who know about corgis and homing pigeons; Danna Schaeffer, best friend and best proofreader, ever; Melanie Cecka, Deb Shapiro, Stacy Cantor, and everyone at Bloomsbury Children's; Kim Witherspoon and David Forrer; Karen Rinaldi; Dawn Stuart and Regina Castillo; and, last but not least, Jerrod Allen, my in-house expert on capacitors, Bluetooth technology, and the mysteries of being an oldest older brother.

A word about the Oregon Humane Society: The Portland Humane Society, where some of this mystery takes place, is based on the Oregon Humane Society. Founded in 1878, OHS is one of the oldest animal shelters in the country. It now serves the needs of over 13,000 animals per year, and has one of the highest animal adoption rates in the country. As Minerva will tell you, the facility is most excellent and the animals well cared for. For more information go to www.oregonhumane.org.